DAWN

DAWN

SELAHATTIN DEMIRTAŞ

Translated from the Turkish
by Amy Marie Spangler and Kate Ferguson

HOGARTH
LONDON · NEW YORK

1 3 5 7 9 10 8 6 4 2

Hogarth, an imprint of Vintage,
20 Vauxhall Bridge Road,
London SW1V 2SA

Hogarth is part of the Penguin Random House group of companies
whose addresses can be found at global.penguinrandomhouse.com

Penguin
Random House
UK

First published by Hogarth in 2019

penguin.co.uk/vintage

A CIP catalogue record for this book is available from the British Library

This book has been selected to receive financial assistance from English PEN's
'PEN Translates' programme, supported by Arts Council English. English PEN
exists to promote literature and our understanding of it, to uphold writers'
freedoms around the world, to campaign against the persecution and imprisonment
of writers for stating their views, and to promote the friendly co-operation
of writers and the free exchange of ideas. www.englishpen.org

Supported using public funding by

**ARTS COUNCIL
ENGLAND**

ISBN 9781781090749

Printed and bound in Great Britain by Clays Ltd, Elcograf S.p.A.

Penguin Random House is committed to a sustainable future
for our business, our readers and our planet. This book is made
from Forest Stewardship Council® certified paper.

MIX
Paper from
responsible sources
FSC® C018179

This book is dedicated to all women
who have been murdered or victims of violence

CONTENTS

FOREWORD

Selahattin Demirtaş has been in prison since November 2016. The official charge is terrorism, a term that President Recep Tayyip Erdoğan has expanded in recent years to cover anything he regards as a political threat. And Demirtaş is indeed a great threat. He is Turkey's voice for peace, not just on behalf of its Kurds but for all those seeking social justice in Turkey through democratic means. Denied his place in the National Assembly, he has nevertheless kept in touch with the outside world by writing fiction.

When he first picked up his pen in his prison cell near

Turkey's western border, he would have known that he was joining a grand tradition. He would have recalled, in the first instance, Turkey's greatest poet, Nâzım Hikmet, who composed his most powerful and enduring works behind bars. He would have thought, too, of Orhan Kemal, chronicler of the dispossessed, who wrote his first fiction under Hikmet's tutelage behind those same bars. He would have taken inspiration from Sevgi Soysal, who wrote with humor and heart about life in a women's political prison, and from Yaşar Kemal, the master of the modern epic, who devoted his life on and off the page (as well as in and out of prison) to those who could imagine a world beyond the injustices of authoritarian rule.

In addition to giving Demirtaş courage, his literary predecessors would also have given him an audience. Running alongside Turkey's grand tradition of writing resistance is a grand tradition of reading it. For the book in your hands is not a political tract. It is a collection of short stories, telling of ordinary people with ordinary lives and drawing out their hopes and fears with compassion and a gentle wit.

Born and raised in the southeastern city of Elazığ, Selahattin Demirtaş was five years old when the newly founded Kurdistan Workers Party (PKK) began its campaign for Kurdish independence. By the time he was eleven the PKK had made its bid for a full-scale Kurdish insurgency. Throughout his teenage years, Demirtaş was a silent witness to the civil conflict that ensued—assaults on the police and the army by the PKK, and mass arrests, widespread use of torture, village clearances, and extrajudicial killings at the hands of the state.

Violence bred violence. In 1991, when Demirtaş was seventeen, a prominent Kurdish activist named Vedat Aydın stood up at a human rights conference in Ankara and caused a furore by addressing his audience in his mother tongue, thereby breaking a language ban that had been in place for more than a decade. Here, at last, was a man seeking a voice for Kurds in the corridors of power. But not, it transpired, for long. It was after Aydın's mutilated body was found in a country field, and Turkish security forces opened fire on the many thousands attending his funeral, that Demirtaş decided to devote his life to the Kurdish cause. After graduating with a law degree from Ankara University, he worked as a human rights lawyer and joined the executive board of the Diyarbakır branch of the Human Rights Association, which Vedat Aydın himself had once headed. Demirtaş soon earned himself the nickname Bones, on account of his dogged commitment to recovering the bodies of PKK fighters and returning them to their families for burial. The undeclared war raged on, with no end in sight.

In 2007, when Demirtaş won his first seat in the National Assembly as an independent, Recep Tayyip Erdoğan had been prime minister for four years. His chief ally was the Islamist cleric Fethullah Gülen, who, though living in exile in rural Pennsylvania, presided over a vast empire of schools, banks, and newspapers, and was believed to have filled the state's institutions with his supporters. Erdoğan's chief adversary was the staunchly secularist military. A protracted power struggle ended with his charging the leadership of the three branches of the armed forces with treason. Most were still incarcerated when the leader of the PKK, also in prison, announced that he was prepared to discuss a cease-fire. As talks progressed, Demirtaş became an increasingly powerful voice, not just at the negotiating table but in public, advocating for peace and a nation in which Turks and Kurds might work together, "arm in arm," as he put it, to "salvage Turkey's crippled democracy."

In 2012 he helped to found the Peoples' Democratic Party (HDP), which soon reached voters well beyond its Kurdish base. Educated Turks, particularly younger ones, were impressed by the party's embrace of cultural and political diversity, its call for peaceful reconciliation, and its commitment to gender equality. This last commitment was reflected in its institutional structure, modeled on the German Green Party's co-leadership system, in which roles were shared between a woman and a man at every level. In 2014, when Demirtaş stepped up to the party's top position, he did so alongside a female colleague, Figen Yüksekdağ. The party's charter also called for an autonomous Women's Congress. Charged with mainstreaming women's concerns, it played a key part in the selection of nominations, encouraging women to step forward and setting their application fee at half the fee set for men.

In June 2015, the Peoples' Democratic Party fought its first general election. It came in fourth, winning 13 percent of the vote and 80 of the Grand National Assembly's 550 seats. This unprecedented victory might have marked a new era in national politics, had it not been complicated by other machinations on the political chessboard. Having cleansed and tamed the army, replacing his old enemies with his own supporters, Erdoğan was becoming steadily more autocratic. Shedding his pluralist rhetoric, he had reverted to the old monolithic nationalism. With this came a growing mistrust of Kurdish ambitions. The conflict in neighboring Syria, and particularly its Kurdish fighters (much admired in the West for holding back ISIS), posed a dangerous example. Once again, tanks rolled into the cities of the Kurdish Southeast. Curfews were imposed, often lasting days, trapping residents in their homes with limited food and water amid gunfire and bombs. As their neighborhoods turned to rubble, they were prevented even from burying their dead.

Back in Ankara, meanwhile, the Islamist alliance had come apart. Following a series of high-profile corruption cases launched by the pro-Gülen judiciary and police against Erdoğan's Justice and Development Party (AKP), the nation's two leading Islamist groups were now bitter political foes.

Then, on July 15, 2016, came one of the most bizarre and bloodiest attempted coups that Turkey—a veteran of unusual coups—has ever seen. Live-streamed from the outset, and foiled within hours, it prompted in Erdoğan a rage that he was quick to take out on his critics, real and perceived. He reasserted state control over the Kurdish regions, meeting any resistance with grotesquely disproportionate force. By November of that year, Demirtaş and other leading members of his party were arrested and accused of spreading propaganda for the PKK, a charge Demirtaş categorically denies.

Three years after the attempted coup, Turkey is the world's largest jailer of journalists. Tens of thousands of civil servants, teachers, and academics have lost their jobs or been subjected to criminal investigations. Outside the public sector, many have suffered the same fate simply for having sent their children to the wrong school or used the wrong bank.

While some of Erdoğan's critics have been able to flee the country, many more have had their passports revoked or been banned from travel. For those branded "traitors" or "terrorists," it has become difficult to find work, and it is now estimated that there are more than a million

Turkish citizens suffering what some are calling "civil death." Shunned by neighbors, barred from employment, and unable to make new lives abroad, they and their families have been left destitute and without recourse.

The Kurdish regions have been hardest hit. "Today, if you go to Kurdish cities," says the author and artist Nurcan Baysal, "you will see police barricades in front of municipal buildings, police stations, and official buildings. You will see tanks, armored vehicles, police, and soldiers with heavy weapons in the streets. You will see demolished cities and homeless people. You will see people living in tents in the rural areas of Şırnak and Hakkâri. You will see thousands of teachers, doctors, academics, writers, and journalists out of work. You will see checkpoints everywhere. Inside the prisons, you will see four to six people trying to sleep in one bed because of how crowded it is." But, as she goes on to point out, the eyes of the world remain closed. Following several high-profile detentions of foreign journalists, very few reporters from the international media can be found in the regions.

Erdoğan now controls all major domestic media outlets. His heavy employment of surveillance technologies means that no one using social media can expect to do so undetected. Nevertheless, since *Dawn* was published in Turkey, in the spring of 2018, it has sold at least 220,000 copies; and when twenty authors stepped in at a recent book fair to sign copies in Demirtaş's absence, the queue was six hours long.

What attracts Turkey's readers to Demirtaş the writer is what drew them to Demirtaş the politician: his humor, his compassion for the common man, his long-standing commitment to women's rights, and his connection with Turkey's younger generation—wired, worldly, and wishing for greater personal and political freedom. But above all, they treasure him for the precious sliver of hope that rises out of every story in this collection, however dark—that despite all the reversals of recent years, there is hope for Turkey's broken democracy, if only Turks and Kurds can learn to work together.

The harshness of life is always there, looming in the margins. But no matter where his characters happen to be—in prison or at the back of a bus, in a cemetery remembering their dead, or in the kitchen apologizing to their mothers—they remain artful and imaginative storytellers, ringing with the music of everyday speech, as they find the strength to keep on going, no matter what. "If you walk with courage and determination," says one, "sometimes you can move faster than a car." "Tough times eventually come to an end, Mother, they always do," says another as he finishes admitting to his many boyhood pranks. "I kiss your hands in gratitude," he adds, "and the hands of mothers everywhere."

These words could strike readers as disingenuous if

they did not know Demirtaş, who has, from the outset, seen women—be they mothers or daughters, workers or professionals, activists or voters—as a powerful force for change. That he also understands the dangers women face in Turkey today is starkly evident in his title story, about an honor killing.

The victim's name is Seher, which means "dawn" in Turkish. But there is no light in this story. There is only the distress of the boy who is made to kill his sister. That he alone of the men will suffer pangs of conscience might not seem to offer his mother and younger sisters much hope, but Demirtaş the writer-politician refuses to lose heart. "Dawn marks the first moments when light emerges from darkness," he said, when asked why he chose this name and this title for his book. "Dawn represents hope, revives itself anew each day. Darkness thinks itself eternal, and just as it believes it has defeated the light, dawn deals the first blow. This is the moment that brings an end to darkness and marks the beginning of light."

The recent presidential election, in June 2018, won and perhaps rigged by Erdoğan, offered Demirtaş one such moment. When his party put him forward as its candidate, he campaigned with tweets disseminated by his family and his lawyer. The high point of his campaign was the speech he delivered from his prison cell during a phone call to his wife. She went on to share it, virally, on social media. Demirtaş won just over 8 percent of the national vote.

That he is currently facing a combined 183-year sentence is a measure, perhaps, of the danger Turkey's president still sees in him. That he can find the peace of mind to sit in his prison cell, writing playful stories about the everyday world from which he is now excluded, is a measure of his spirit. We cannot know how long he will have to endure this injustice. In the meantime, we have his words, and his promise: to carry on writing; to celebrate the humanity we all share; to seek connection, through translation, with readers in other parts of the world who are also struggling with despots and fanatics; and to remind us that dawn will be waiting on the far side of the horizon.

Maureen Freely
London, November 2018

PREFACE

I write this as a political prisoner in a high-security prison in Edirne, Turkey. I imagine most of you will have never received a letter from prison before, so I would like you to think of this preface as just that: a letter written to you from prison.

I was arrested one year and ten months ago while I was a member of the Turkish parliament and the co-leader of the Peoples' Democratic Party, known as the HDP, for which nearly six million people voted in Turkey's last election. I am among the tens of thousands of dissidents who have been targeted by punitive measures normalized under the state of emergency. The government has so far started 102 investigations and filed 34 separate court cases against me. All in all, I currently face 183 years in prison.

In Western countries, prison is generally thought of as a place where people are punished for their crimes. In Turkey, however, it is a different matter. Behind these walls, there is now a considerable population of qualified and educated people who could serve the needs of any modern, moderate-sized country. As a human rights lawyer—one who has tirelessly reported rights violations in Turkey's prisons for a number of years—it is with complete certainty and considerable sorrow that I tell you that, since becoming a lawyer in 1998, I have never known rights to be abused as frequently and consistently as they are now. Turkey has become a country in which those who stand up to the rising authoritarianism in the government—dissidents who share tweets considered critical of the current regime, university students who wave protest banners, journalists who truthfully report the news, academics who sign petitions calling for peace, and members of parliament acting in the public interest— quickly find themselves incarcerated. The government believes that this policy of collective punishment will suppress the millions of dissidents "on the outside," who are living in a semi-open prison as it is. And so in the nearly two years that I have been imprisoned, there has never been any question in my mind as to why I am here. Like many other dissidents held in Turkey's prisons, I, too, am paying a necessary price in the name of peace and democratization. Yet even if I were forced to spend my entire life behind bars, my belief in the right to defend peace, democracy, and human rights would not waver.

In today's world, literature and politics are thought of as two separate realms, yet I've never subscribed to this view. What readers or voters expect from the writer and politician are, in essence, the same: to be inspired. Both are expected to create meaning and to observe their societies closely and reflect upon the issues that those societies face. Ultimately there is little difference, particularly in oppressive regimes, between the responsibility borne by politicians and that borne by intellectuals who prioritize the good of society.

The truth is, I have always believed, both as a politician and as a writer, that our struggle must be carried out on two levels. The first is an intellectual struggle fought in the field of language, an area that naturally includes literature. We do this in order to reclaim the concepts of peace, democracy, and human rights, concepts that are being eroded day by day, caught as they are within the insincere boundaries of governments and institutional politics. It is said these concepts are what differentiate the developed world from oppressive regimes, West from East, yet in Western governments they are all too often sacrificed at the altar of political and economic interests. This is precisely what lies at the heart of the political crises raging throughout the world as I write.

Today we find ourselves grappling with a political discourse twisted beyond recognition, with political demands forcefully silenced in the name of peace and stability, and regimes that rig elections and trample on civil liberties labeled as "developing democracies." Some may think it naive to turn our attention to the role of literature in the midst of such troubles. I would beg to differ. Literature—the art form that arguably comprises the backbone of any culture—not only remains at the vanguard of critical thinking but also serves as a catalyst for the thoughts and feelings that in turn create political change. Let us not forget that as long as we continue to breathe life into words, those words will not abandon us.

We must restore to literature its transformative role. We have the capability to create a new language around the concepts of peace, democracy, and human rights, and the values inherent to each. But to do so, political activism alone is not enough: We must also engage intellectually and artistically. And so it is by discovering a new way of speaking that we can combat the rise of populism in developed countries, and the authoritarian regimes that are increasing in both number and severity throughout the rest of the world. Yet if we are sincere in our mission, we must also start by being honest with ourselves. For it is not just government policies that are to blame for the crisis of democracy, but societies themselves, which are insufficiently organized and therefore unable to balance the power of governments.

In many countries today, and especially in the Middle East, the constraints of gender, religion, and ethnic identities weigh heavily upon us. As a means of survival, we become withdrawn. Shackled by society, we begin to isolate ourselves. What we need are new forms of struggle that allow us to tear down the walls that hold us in. Yet it is impossible for us to decide alone just how this new method of resistance should take shape.

Creativity is a collaborative process. Throughout history, the fight for justice and equality owes its innovation to the interaction of ideas, emotions, and collective action. In other words, it is the deeds of men and women, unafraid to make sacrifices for the sake of progressive politics and receptive to new ideas, that have changed the world. Despite the issues that face us today, democracy remains alive and well in many countries. And those institutions responsible for keeping democracy alive, that foster peace and protect human rights, did not arise spontaneously. They were built on a history of social struggle rife with sacrifice and negotiation. Just as the women's movement has faced numerous pressures throughout history as it transformed from one wave

to the next, and just as the civil rights movement paid
dearly to dismantle racially discriminatory policies, those
people under authoritarian regimes today are paying a
high price, too, for freedom and democracy. It is up to
us to create a new path founded on a nonviolent belief in
civil resistance, which does not hesitate to make sacrifices
in the fight against oppressive policies. And so, too,
must we create a universal language of politics that will
speak to the hearts and minds of those living both in the
developed world and under authoritarian regimes. I truly
believe that it will be the women, the young, and the
oppressed people of both the East and the West who will
lead the fight to end injustice and inequality and be the
creators of this new language.

This book is a collection of stories about everyday
people, written by a politician fighting for freedom
and equality, after being unjustly imprisoned by an
authoritarian regime. It contains short fragments from
my own past, which have resurfaced in my memory
while I've been here in prison. Most politicians believe
they speak great truths with their lengthy, grandiose
statements. I, on the other hand, have always believed
in the power of human stories. I am trapped inside
these four walls, but I know that there are thousands of
Demirtaşes right now, working the fields. Demirtaş is
down in the mines, at the factories. He is in lecture halls,
in the squares, at the rallies. He is on the construction

sites, at strikes, in the resistance. He has just been fired. Demirtaş is unemployed and poor. He is young, he is a woman, he is a child. He is Turkish, he is Kurdish, he is Circassian. He is Alawite. He is Sunni. No matter who he is, his spirits remain high, his hope intact. What lies at the heart of my relationship with politics is not lofty ideals or abstractions, but ordinary people: ordinary people who are capable of changing the world.

Selahattin Demirtaş
Edirne High–Security Prison, Turkey
August 17, 2018

THE MAN INSIDE

Our prison courtyard is little more than a concrete pen, only four meters wide and eight long. At the same time, it's endless. You could walk it from morning to night without ever getting anywhere. Only two of us occupy this courtyard: myself and my fellow MP, Abdullah Zeydan. But that doesn't mean it's ours alone. This is a communal space, after all, and so we're obliged to honor the rights of the ants and the spiders with which we share it. *They* are the ones who act like they own the place, as if the prison had been built on top of their nests,

and they wouldn't be wrong about that. Still, Abdullah
and I are perfect gentlemen and, all things considered,
the atmosphere is one of mutual respect.

The collective struggle of the ants is a sight to behold.
With spirit and purpose, the entire colony strives
toward the same goal, quietly building a glorious life for
themselves in a gloomy corner of the prison courtyard.
The spiders, on the other hand, are a different beast
altogether. They don't do much of anything. And they're
not exactly social creatures either. Try to engage one in
conversation and he'll soon lose the thread. Or, rather, he
won't actually lose it; he'll just run off with it and use it to
spin his own web.

And then there are the sparrows. A pair of them
settled beneath the eaves of the prison roof to build their
nest. For days they flew back and forth, straw and twigs
in their beaks. Needless to say, it was the female who
did most of the work. The male could occasionally be
seen strutting about with a twig or two, but for the most
part, he'd be preening himself on the barbed wire at the
entrance to their nest. I shouldn't be too hard on him
though, perhaps he was just doing his job.

It took them almost ten days to build their home. We
helped as much as we could, leaving bread crumbs and
water out for them on the window ledge. One day, the
female sparrow flew over to me and said, "*Abi,* God bless
you. If it were up to that worthless man of mine, we'd

have gone hungry long ago. I'd have had to put food on the table besides everything else."

Taken aback, I asked her, "Are you talking to me, *bacı*?"

"I am," she replied. "So you can understand me?"

I nodded, scarcely able to believe my ears. It seems I hadn't entirely forgotten "bird speak," that gibberish we used as kids.

"Don't mention it, ma'am. With all the building and moving, we didn't want to have you worrying about food, too," I said. "Just let us know if you ever need anything. After all, we're neighbors now."

"Thanks, *abi*," she said. And at that very moment, the male sparrow emerged from the nest.

"Who you talking to, woman?"

"Oh, no one," she called back. "I was just thanking our neighbor for the food."

"Get inside!" he screeched. Deciding it was best to let this one slide, the female sparrow retreated into the nest; it wasn't worth the effort. Her mate glared at me menacingly.

"What do you want? Something I can do for you?"

"No, *abi,* I was just asking your wife if you needed—"

"If you have something to say," he snapped, "you say it to *me,* okay?"

"Okay, *abi,* have a good day now," I said, closing the window.

A few days later, we discovered that the female sparrow was about to become a mother: She had laid two eggs in her nest. Our neighbors would be having twins; not identical, but twins all the same. I hope they don't take after their father, I thought. Actually, raw eggs are forbidden here in prison. Cooked ones are fine, but then they don't hatch. It just goes to show: They can ban anything they like, life will always prevail, even in here. It was now clear that our lady friend had been expecting chicks the whole time she was building that nest. Meanwhile her mate had done nothing but swagger around with a scowl on his face.

One morning I woke to a clamor coming from the sparrows' nest. The door to the courtyard had yet to be opened. We have a better view of the nest from our cell anyway, so I got up and walked over to the window to see what was going on. The shouts rose to a deafening pitch.

"Please, not the tear gas!" a voice cried out. From the commotion, you'd have thought the riot police had come to break up a protest. Four male sparrows had surrounded the nest. They chirped aggressively at our neighbors, who were putting up a desperate fight to protect their home.

As far as I could make out, these newcomers were inspectors from the Department of Nesting Code Enforcement.

"Look here!" one of them shouted, his tone official.

From his puffed-up feathers, he seemed to be the one in charge. "You built this nest without a permit! No ifs or buts about it. Either we tear it down now or we'll be back to seize one of those chicks as a fine!" he threatened, gesturing toward the eggs.

"That's right," the other three echoed. "No ifs or buts about it!"

Wings raised in defiance, the female sparrow blocked the entrance to the nest.

"Take my home? Take my baby? Over my dead body!"

"Yes, over her dead body!" her mate chimed in, though it was unclear whether he was protesting or asking for a favor.

The chief and his demolition team were closing in on the nest.

"I won't tell you again," the chief said. "Either you obey the law or I throw you both in prison."

At these words, the couple turned to me. Our eyes met. They seemed to be asking, "What do you think, neighbor? What should we do now?" I looked at them as if to say, "Well, if you ask me, I'd say don't back down."

"I'll never surrender, no matter what!" the female sparrow declared.

"That's my girl!" the male added, more assertively this time. "Don't you ever surrender, no matter what!"

Then, just like that, the female launched herself at the inspectors.

Pandemonium erupted within the barbed-wire of the prison yard. A lone female sparrow standing up to four state officials! As this extraordinary feat of resistance unfolded, her partner hopped about nervously on the sidelines. "Please, kind sir," he groveled, "please, would you stop? Wait a minute, sir, there's no need for a fuss. Two chicks is one too many for us anyway."

At this, the female sparrow shot him a withering glance and he shrank deep into his feathers. I'm not exaggerating: She stood her ground for a good ten minutes until she had single-handedly chased off those four state officials, showing astounding resolve in the face of attack and successfully protecting her eggs and nest. Meanwhile, my fellow male had gone back to his usual ways. Now he was glaring at me.

"Don't you look at me like that, Hamza," I said (I'd decided to call him Hamza, by the way). "First things first: Kill the man inside you, my friend, that's what you've got to do."

Hamza's blank stare said nothing. And to this day, he's still keeping quiet on the matter. Should there be any further developments, though, I'll be sure to write and let you know.

SEHER

On the night before *bayram,* Seher made henna paste. Her little sisters had drawn red circles on their palms and gloved their hands in old socks, then curled up on the mattress she'd laid out for them on the floor. After she had hennaed her own hands, Seher joined them. Pınar and Kader were too excited to sleep. Pınar couldn't stop thinking about her new dress and delighted at the thought of herself in it—the first new dress she had ever owned. Until then, she had always made do with Kader's hand-me-downs. Kader had a new pair of shoes for *bayram* and was no less excited than Pınar. They lay awake, giggling under the quilt late into the night, paying no heed to their *abla*'s stern words. They knew perfectly well that Seher was only bluffing since she could never truly be angry with them. Seher held them until, exhausted, they had both fallen asleep.

Something else kept Seher awake that night. Earlier in the day, at the end of their shift, she and Hayri had made plans to meet at a local café. Hayri and Seher worked together at the same textile factory, and as it was the eve of *bayram,* they'd been let out of work early. As they were leaving, Hayri had approached her and bashfully asked her on a date. The truth was, Seher had been expecting this. They had been stealing glances at each other for some time and were already the subject of gossip at work. Their colleagues were quick to pick up on such things.

At twenty-two, Seher, along with everyone else, thought her chances of marriage were almost behind her, and she was beginning to worry about being left on the shelf. Other girls her age had married before they had even turned eighteen and were already having children. A few suitors had asked for Seher's hand, but she had managed to convince her family they weren't a good match. Now, though, she had fallen for Hayri. Tall, with wavy hair and full lips, he could even be considered handsome. They had been working together for almost eight months; Hayri had been hired after completing his

military service, while Seher had been at the factory for
four years.

The sisters woke early to cheerful commotion as the
family threw themselves into the day. Seher's father,
Gani, her brother Hâdi, three years her senior, and her
fifteen-year-old brother, Engin, left for the mosque for
bayram prayers. As soon as they were gone, Pınar and
Kader ran to the bathroom to wash the dried henna from
their hands. Only the thrill of a festive *bayram* morning
could put children in such good spirits at this early hour.
After scrubbing her own hands, Seher made sure her
sisters' hands, now stained red as pomegranates, were
good and clean, too. Seher breathed in the familiar scent
of henna before kissing their tiny palms.

Their mother, Sultan, was busy in the kitchen
preparing breakfast for when the men of the house
returned from the mosque. As Seher helped her mother,
the little ones rushed off to don their *bayram* outfits. The
mattresses in both rooms were put away and the meal laid
out on the floor. It was only during *bayram* that the family
sat down together for breakfast, and once the men had
returned, everyone exchanged holiday greetings. First
each of them kissed the hand of Gani *Baba*. He embraced
only Pınar and Kader, though, before giving them their
bayram spending money. Then the children kissed their
mother's hand, and she in turn hugged them warmly
and smothered them in kisses. As the brothers and sisters

threw their arms around one another, Pınar and Kader managed to wrangle some more money out of their eldest brother, Hâdi. Although she knew it made him squirm, Seher hugged and kissed her little brother, Engin, too. Usually he would have made a fuss, but it was *bayram,* and it was his Seher *Abla* who was doing the kissing. Engin adored his older sister, and she doted on him in return. And though he was too old for it, she took out her purse and gave him some *bayram* spending money. At first Engin refused to take it, but Seher insisted until he relented, returning her affection. The whole family then sat down to eat, brimming with talk and excitement.

By the afternoon, the traditional *bayram* visits with the neighbors were over and the men had all left, each going about his own business. In just three hours it would be time for Seher's date with Hayri, but she still hadn't told her mother of her plans. While Sultan *Ana* was devoted to all of her children, Seher held a special place in her heart. She wasn't only her daughter, she was her friend and confidante, too, and Sultan *Ana* was much easier on her than on her other children. And so when Seher finally told her mother she was going out, she did not object. She didn't ask any questions, though she knew her daughter well enough to guess. She only told her to be careful.

Seher and Hayri were to meet at the café across from the Adana Courthouse. As Seher walked in, she saw

Hayri sitting alone at a table. "Welcome, and happy *bayram,*" he said, standing up and taking her hand.

"Thank you, and happy *bayram* to you, too," she replied, a tremble in her voice. She had broken into a nervous sweat. It was the first time she'd been on a date and she had no idea what to say or do. For years, her life had consisted of nothing but the monotony of work and domestic life. Sometimes the girls in the factory would speak of such things as dating, but experiencing it herself was altogether different. Unlike Seher, Hayri seemed calm and collected. He kept the conversation turning until Seher's pounding heart settled back in her chest. They talked about their families and their pasts, and Seher soon grew more comfortable. She felt safe, as if she and Hayri had known each other for years. This was mostly due to Hayri. The more he talked, the more he entranced her. He clearly knew what he was doing. It was only to be expected; Hayri was, after all, a man. He had probably been out with other girls before. But right now it was *her* he was charming, and that was all that mattered. When he spoke, Hayri lowered his head, giving Seher the chance to take a long look at him. By the time they left the café two hours later, she could barely feel the ground beneath her feet. So this, she thought, must be love. As she made her way back to her home in Şakirpaşa, all she could think of was Hayri.

Her cheeks were flushed and her head was spinning. But as she neared home, the enchantment of her clandestine meeting gave way to fear. If her father and Hâdi heard about this, they'd break her legs. She would have to be careful not to give anything away. She couldn't even share this secret with her mother—not yet. When she arrived back home, her father and brothers still hadn't returned. Her mother chose not to ask any questions; she knew Seher would tell her when the time was right.

That night, they laid out the mattresses early. Worn out by the day's excitement, Pınar and Kader fell asleep the moment their heads touched the pillow. Seher took her place beside them but lay awake for hours dreaming of Hayri, imagining their future together, their wedding, the dress she would wear. . . . She pictured their house, the furniture they'd have. She thought of herself in the house, alone with Hayri, and a blush rose to her cheeks. Eventually, she, too, fell asleep.

The next morning the family sat down to breakfast again. The festive mood of the first day of *bayram* had subsided, but all were still in good cheer. Seher, though, couldn't look anyone in the eye, for fear of revealing her secret. Gani *Baba* and Hâdi *Abi* were also avoiding each other's gaze that morning. The previous night they had crossed paths in the Adana brothel but then gone their separate ways, pretending not to have seen each other. Both knew, however, that they had. Now they were obliged to act as if nothing had happened—such was the unspoken pact between men in these situations. Still, they couldn't bring themselves to look at, let alone speak to, each other. Hâdi had been engaged for over a year and talk of his wedding that summer made the two of them even more uncomfortable.

Back at work after the *bayram,* Seher couldn't stop her heart from racing. All morning long, she kept glancing over at Hayri. Then, at lunch, the two of them sat together in the canteen. Measuring him against the other men in the factory, she couldn't believe her luck. Hayri was surely the kindest, most handsome among them, and of all the girls in the factory, he had chosen her. She felt as though she were living a fairy tale, and she wanted that feeling to last forever.

At the end of the day, they left work together. When Seher went to say goodbye, Hayri lowered his eyes. "Some friends are coming to pick me up," he said. "We can drive you home if you like."

"No, that's okay," Seher replied, "I wouldn't want you to go out of your way."

"It's no trouble at all, we're heading in that direction."

Seher allowed herself to be persuaded. "All right then, but just drop me off at the end of the road."

Hayri seemed to understand. "Sure, we'll drop you off wherever you want."

As they got in the car, Hayri greeted his friends

without introducing her to them. The two men in the front exchanged a few words in a low whisper. As they drove, Hayri barely spoke to Seher and he didn't tell the driver where they were to take her. Dusk had fallen by the time they turned off the main road at the Balcalı exit.

"You're going the wrong way!" Seher called out, now a little worried. "I live in Şakirpaşa."

Hayri sought to placate her. "Don't worry, we're just going for a ride around the dam, get some air, then we'll take you home. It'll be nice to do something different for a change, right?"

"Sure," said Seher, a note of concern in her voice, "but we mustn't be too late, my family will be expecting me."

The car took a sharp turn down a forest road. Seher's heart pounded in her ears. They drove through the forest for some time before stopping.

"Let's go for a little walk. The forest air will do us good," said Hayri.

"No, I don't want to," Seher replied, afraid now, "I have to get home."

Gripping her arm forcefully, Hayri dragged her from the car. "Then why the hell did you get in to begin with?"

Seher couldn't tell which of them had spoken. This voice couldn't belong to Hayri.

The other two men got out of the car and walked

around. One grabbed Seher from behind while the other seized a fistful of her hair. With Hayri's help, they forced her to the ground. One pinned her down by her feet, the other by her wrists. She couldn't breathe. She tried to scream, but no sound escaped her throat. The world stopped, everything came to a standstill. The only thing moving was Hayri.

When she came to at the side of a road, she first thought she was in a dream. She tried to rouse herself, only to find she was already awake. Her clothes were torn, her legs covered in blood. I must have been hit by a car, she thought. That must have been what happened. The accident must have knocked her out and everything else was just a nightmare. That's what she told herself. The street was quiet. She was in an industrial area, but where exactly she couldn't tell. She walked toward the sound of cars until she came to the main road and paused to find her bearings; she wasn't far from home. She began to walk again, trying to block out her thoughts.

Sultan *Ana* opened the door and at the sight of Seher let out a cry. "What happened to you? What happened, my love?" she asked, again and again, gathering her daughter into her arms.

Seher couldn't answer, the words stuck in her throat.

Her father and brothers hadn't arrived home yet. They ran a vegetable stand at the local market, leaving early each morning and returning late. Pınar and Kader looked on, eyes wide with fear, as their mother led their sister into the bathroom.

Sultan *Ana* gently undressed Seher, and when she saw her daughter's body, bloody and bruised, she couldn't hold back the tears. She buried her face in Seher's hair and wept. The tears from her eyes fell into the hot water that she ladled over her daughter. She bathed Seher in those tears. Combing her hair over and over, she washed her once more. Seher had at last begun to emerge from her daze. The street filled with a harrowing cry, the first sound to escape her lips for hours. Knowing what had happened and what was to follow, mother and daughter held each other tightly and wept.

Sultan *Ana* wrapped Seher in a towel before putting on her pajamas, then laid her down and pulled the quilt around her. She sat by her side, stroking her hair and reciting prayers. Pınar and Kader watched them soundlessly from the corner of the room. Seher slept. A sweet, peaceful sleep, like a baby in her mother's arms, the only expression on her face one of fatigue. Sultan *Ana* rose gently from her daughter's side and led her two youngest children out of the room.

A short while later there was a loud knock at the door. The men had returned. The neighbors had called and told them something was wrong. Some had seen Seher on the street covered in blood, others had heard the screams coming from the house. Alarmed, the men had rushed home.

"What happened to Seher?" asked Gani *Baba*.

Sultan *Ana* evaded his question. "She's sleeping, she's fine."

"Tell me, what happened?" he pressed.

"What difference does it make?" Sultan *Ana* replied, her head held high. "It's over now."

Gani *Baba* and Hâdi stood motionless as the reality sank in; Engin, still just a boy, had yet to understand what was unfolding.

Gani *Baba* turned to Hâdi. "Call your uncles, tell them to come straight over," he said firmly.

"It's too late to call anyone now. Let's wait until morning," Sultan *Ana* urged, "tomorrow's a new day."

"No good will come from waiting," Gani *Baba* replied. "What's done is done."

Sultan *Ana* threw herself at her husband's feet. "It's not her fault, Gani. My poor innocent child! Spare her, Gani, please," she begged him. But her husband refused to be swayed.

Two of Seher's uncles, Gani *Baba*'s older brothers, lived nearby, and it wasn't long before they arrived. The men shut themselves away in a room for some time, debating. Sultan *Ana* stayed by her daughter's side, silent tears falling from her eyes as she stroked Seher's hair and breathed in her scent. The uncles left without saying a word.

Hâdi came into the room where Seher was sleeping. "*Ana,* you need to leave," he said.

Resolute, Sultan *Ana* stood up to her son. "No. I will not forsake my daughter. Wherever you're taking her, take me, too."

"Stay out of this! It has nothing to do with you. It's *our* honor that's at stake," said Hâdi.

"To hell with your honor," cried Sultan *Ana.* "My Seher is innocent, don't you lay a finger on her."

Seher, still only half conscious, opened her eyes and met her brother's gaze. Their eyes filled with tears, yet Hâdi's face remained stern. Seher knew what was to come.

She stood up slowly and went to the bathroom. After getting dressed, she returned to her mother's side and asked her brother to let her say her goodbyes. Hâdi left the room. Seher and her mother held each other, sobbing, unable to speak. Pınar and Kader, too, were afraid, and in tears. Seher hugged her little sisters, pressing her face into their hair, and kissed them.

"Don't ever forget your *abla,* okay?"

The young girls couldn't grasp what was happening but sensed it was serious; they clung to their sister, unwilling to let her go.

"Enough now, we're leaving," Gani *Baba* ordered.

Sultan *Ana* put herself between her daughter and her husband. "You'll have to kill me first!"

Gani *Baba* slapped her with such force that she fell to the floor, and with a volley of curses he ordered her out of the way. Sultan *Ana* clung to her husband's feet, pleading and wringing her hands, but it was no use; her pleas went unheard. Without looking Seher in the face, Gani *Baba* gestured toward the door. Seher lowered her head and walked out. The truck stood waiting at the front of the house, and one by one they got in. Neighbors peered out from behind their curtains to watch as Seher was taken away.

No one uttered a word for the entire journey. Seher sat next to Engin in the backseat, gripping his hand. Were it not for fear of their father, Engin would have wrapped his arms around his sister. They pulled over by an empty field on the outskirts of the city. Seher got out first and waited for the others. Her face shone in the light of the moon, graceful and sublime. They walked in single file toward the middle of the field—Gani *Baba,* followed by Seher, then Hâdi, with Engin at the rear. The harsh Adana frost had frozen the earth; the crunch of their footsteps was the only sound to be heard. When their father stopped, those behind him did, too. Gani *Baba* turned, took the gun from his belt, and held it out to Engin. And then, for the first time, Seher lost her composure.

"*Baba,* I beg of you, don't do this to Engin. He's just a child, he won't last in prison, *Baba.* Let me do it myself, don't sacrifice Engin because of me, *Baba.*"

Fighting back his tears, Gani *Baba* said sternly, "Go on, take it, son. Take it, Engin, get it over with."

Engin reached out and took the gun from his father's hand, eyes wide with shock and fear. He was only a child. The night was cold and the gun was heavy; his hand shook.

"Get down on your knees!" Hâdi *Abi* ordered Seher, trying to control the emotion in his voice.

Seher turned to her father. With the last of her energy she implored him, "Please, let me kiss your hand, *Baba.*"

Gani *Baba* held out his hand. Seher brought it to her lips and then to her forehead. "Forgive my sins against you, Father."

"They are forgiven, my daughter," her father responded, wiping his eyes. "Forgive mine, too."

"They are forgiven," said Seher. She turned and embraced Hâdi, asking also for his forgiveness. Hâdi maintained his stony silence. Finally, she embraced Engin. He placed the gun on the ground and held on to his sister. Seher kissed him over and over again, breathing him in one last time.

Seher knelt on the ground, and Engin picked up the gun and held it to the back of his sister's head. The gun shook.

"Engin, my dear sweet Engin," said Seher. "Don't be afraid, baby brother," she continued, giving him the courage he needed. "Don't be afraid, not of anything or anyone. And you look after yourself in prison."

Engin closed his eyes tightly. "Seher *Abla*!" he cried. His voice was soon joined by the crack of gunshot. A flock of crows took flight from the poplars in the distance. Seher fell forward. Her warm blood met the frozen earth of Çukurova, flowing over the ice and the henna on her hand.

One evening in a forest, three men robbed Seher of her dreams.

One night in an empty field, three men robbed Seher of her life.

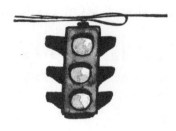

NAZAN THE CLEANING LADY

That Renault station wagon you see over there, it's from our neighborhood—and so are all the guys inside it. They're Halime *Teyze*'s boys. The one at the steering wheel is Yusuf, he's the oldest. Three of the others are his brothers, and next to them is cousin Muhittin, and that little squirt in the back is Muhittin's son, Süleyman. They do fancy plastering on ceilings, that's what all the stuff in the back is for. They make a fine team and work like demons—but the work's never steady. It's Yusuf who gets the gigs, as most of the subcontractors know him. He's a reliable guy, with a good head on his shoulders. He dropped out of middle school and is now engaged to Süheyla, who's also from our neighborhood. Süheyla is Orhan's daughter; Orhan's a retired janitor.

The light just turned green—we're off! Süleyman catches sight of me in the bus at the very last moment and waves. I wave back.

My name is Nazan. I'm eighteen. I finished middle school but then had to drop out. I've got two little sisters, Nebile and Gülbahar. It was our mother who brought us up. My father worked for the city of Ankara, here in Mamak, but he died when I was five. They say he was a first-rate mechanic. He was underneath a bus at the city garage one day, working on the engine, when the jack tipped over. My mother was eight months pregnant at the time. He left us with a widow's pension and a collection of car magazines. He had a real passion for cars, never missed an issue of those magazines, and even went through all the newspapers, cutting out pictures of cars he liked. His dream car was a black Mustang. He put up a poster of one on the kitchen wall. He always told my mother that he was going to buy a car of his own someday. She never did take down that Mustang poster; it's still hanging there today. So you see, I grew up reading my father's car magazines, and that's where *my* passion for cars comes from.

Turns out a widow's pension wasn't enough to live on

and so my mother took on a job as a housecleaner. After I dropped out of school, I'd sometimes tag along and help her out. When I did, we'd leave my sisters with our neighbor, Hasret. Once I'd learned to do it well enough myself, I told my mother that it was my turn, that she didn't have to work anymore. And so I've been cleaning houses for a year now.

Our house is in Mamak's *gecekondu* neighborhood, where everyone knows one another. We're all poor, so no one sticks out as being worse off than the next. It's really only when we go downtown that the truth slaps us in the face. I take the bus to work, and I always sit by the window. I just love watching all the passing cars and the people in them, especially when we've stopped at a red light or are stuck in traffic. For instance, that's Haydar *Amca* in the '86 Fargo next to us right now. He'll haul anything in that truck—when he can find work, that is. You can usually find him parked at the top of the street, on the corner of the main road. He's from Çorum and has two daughters, both university students. His wife, Besime *Teyze*, is bedridden; she was hit by a car three years ago. The guy who did it just drove off, left her there for dead. One of their girls was arrested last year at a student demo on the anniversary of Madımak.

The light just turned green.

You can always tell which people and which cars are from our neighborhood. They have so much in common.

They're all overworked, run-down, scruffy old things; they reek of poverty and grip the steering wheel with both hands like it's their bread and butter. When you reach the main road, the cars start changing and so do the people inside them. All of a sudden you start seeing civil servants and businessmen, women drivers, and handsome young men, too. The cars here are all newer than the ones in our neighborhood. Just take that couple in the gray Passat next to us: I reckon they both have jobs. Maybe she works at a bank; he looks like he's a manager somewhere. Perhaps he's going to drop her off at the bank first, then head to work himself. I'd say they've been married a long time and they're riding in the same car only because they have to. They exchange a few words every now and then, but without looking at each other. My guess is they're still together out of a sense of duty. They took out a loan to buy the car and they're both paying off the installments, but the man's acting like it's his and his alone—that's the advantage of being at the steering wheel, I suppose.

We're on the move again and now here's a white Şahin next to us. Somebody did a crappy job remodeling it. The four guys inside aren't from our neighborhood, but they're definitely from our side of the tracks. Looks like they're on their way to work. They're the kind of guys who go cruising around on the weekends, just to show off. In the opposite lane there's a maroon BMW 740—

now that's one fabulous car. The couple whose house I clean, they have the same one. They even have the same license plate. Hey, hold on a second. . . . Well, if that isn't Murat *Bey* himself! But the woman next to him, she's not Sevgi *Hanım*. Must be a friend from work or something. Good lord, he just kissed her on the lips.

The light's green again.

That can't be right, I didn't see what I think I saw or, better yet, I didn't see anything at all. Sevgi *Hanım*'s a doctor; she works at a hospital in the emergency department. And Murat *Bey* owns a construction company. They've been married for four years now and don't have any children, but they're super fond of each other, or at least they *were*. Kızılay Square's been closed off to traffic. I've got to get off the bus now and I have no choice but to walk. I'll need to catch another bus from the other side of the square. Sevgi *Hanım* and her husband live on the thirteenth floor of a fancy building in Çukurambar. I clean their place twice a week. They pay me well, God bless them.

There must be some kind of demonstration happening in Kızılay, I can smell the tear gas from here. My eyes are burning, and it's getting harder and harder to breathe. Everyone around me is coughing and choking, running this way and that. Should I make a run for it, too? I'd better cross over and take the back streets.

Ow! Something hard has just hit me in the head, probably cracked my skull open. I'm on the ground and feel like I'm suffocating. Is this the end of the road for me? Perhaps it is, I tell myself, but why am I dying? Why now? And who's killing me? I suppose I'll have to leave those questions to the living. I've fallen flat on my face, so my nose is probably broken, too. I'm sitting in the middle of the road, watching all that is going on around me, and it's almost too real to be true. My nose is bleeding; I can taste the blood in my mouth. There are women being dragged by the hair, young protesters trying to yell out slogans as they're beaten with batons, people throwing stones, others wielding signs to fend off the blows, tanks, water cannons, sirens, sirens . . .

I find myself in an ambulance, wearing an oxygen mask. There are other wounded people in here, too. They're all standing up though; it's only me who's on a stretcher. There are three paramedics or maybe one of them's a doctor. One of the paramedics is a young man with slicked-back hair, not what I'd call handsome. But I bet he squanders all his money on his looks. Probably doesn't have a car, but he's got plenty of hair gel. The female paramedic isn't as flashy. All the time she's taking care of us, she rants on about the bastards who did this. She's obviously a union member; her face is angry, but her eyes are full of kindness. Every now and then she asks me if I'm all right. I nod to say that I am. She doesn't own a car, but she's married, so maybe her husband has one. The doctor is a woman, younger than either of the paramedics. They keep trying to get her attention. "Doctor, Doctor!" But she's in such a panic that she's forgotten she is even a doctor. I'd say she's single, doesn't have a car, either. That union member, though, now she's got a cool head; she's the real boss here.

We've arrived, I think. The ambulance door opens and they whisk me to the emergency department. The two guys wheeling me in on the stretcher seem calm and collected. They're not from our neighborhood, but they're definitely from our side of the tracks. They're both bachelors; one of them might even own a secondhand motorcycle. They must have done this a thousand times already; they could probably do it with their eyes closed. From the way they call out, ordering everyone out of their way, you'd think they were hotshot surgeons or something. *They're* probably the bosses around here. The emergency department is packed, full of people moaning in pain and screaming. The two "surgeons" lift me up just like that and place me on a bed, then they grab the empty stretcher and take off again.

I lie there for a while, waiting. I touch the back of my head, figure my brains must have oozed out of my skull. But when I look at my hand, expecting to see a glob of bloody brains on it, there's nothing. I check again, feeling around carefully this time. Turns out my head wasn't split open after all; there's a good-sized bump on it, though, about as big as my fist.

A bunch of medics in white coats flock to my side. They dart around so quickly that I can't tell one from the other. They're all young, unmarried, medical-student types. Not one of them has a car.

"Ma'am, this patient's taken a blow to the head and she may have a broken nose," one of them says. The doctor they call "ma'am" leans over to get a closer look at me. Our eyes meet.

"Sevgi *Hanım*!" I cry.

She gives me a blank look. "I'm sorry. Do I know you?" My face must be a real mess, otherwise she would have recognized me.

"It's me, Nazan," I cry.

"My God, Nazan! What happened to you?"

I shrug my shoulders as if to say, "Don't ask me."

"Okay, I see," she says. "Take her on over to radiology."

They bring me back after I've had my X-rays done. Sevgi *Hanım* stands next to me while she looks them over. "Well, at least there's nothing serious—nothing broken, no fractures, no internal bleeding. You're going to have to spend the night here, though, and we'll take another

X-ray tomorrow. They're going to dress your wounds now and put you on an IV; it'll help with the pain," she says.

"But my mother," I reply, "I need to call my mother."

"Don't worry, I'll let her know," she says. Just then a group of police officers show up, all holding walkie-talkies.

"Which ones were brought in from the demonstration?" they ask.

No one answers.

The police chief gets angry. "Who's in charge here?" he shouts.

Sevgi *Hanım* steps forward. "I am."

The chief asks again which of us were brought in from the demonstration.

"We have no way of knowing," she answers, adding, "Our job is to treat people. It makes no difference to us who they are."

The chief glares at her. "Collect all their IDs," he orders the other officers.

Sevgi *Hanım* tries to stop them. "Would you please leave," she says. "We need to finish treating these patients. Let us get on with our job, then you can come back and do yours."

"Take down the doctor's name, too," the chief orders menacingly.

Sevgi *Hanım* comes and stands by my bed. When
one of the officers asks to see my identity card, she tells
him, "She's my cleaning lady, she fell off a ladder while
cleaning." The officer seems convinced; he's very young,
with a look of poverty in his eyes, and almost certainly
doesn't have a car.

The chief yells out from the other side of the room,
"Take her ID, too!" He obviously grew up poor,
but thanks to his car—probably a Ford Mondeo,
secondhand—he's managed to pull ahead, though only
just. Sevgi *Hanım* starts to object. The chief cuts her off.
"There's nothing to worry about, ma'am. If what you say
is true, there won't be any problem now, will there?" But
his tone implies otherwise.

Sevgi *Hanım* turns back to face me. "Everything's
going to be fine, give them your ID. I'll call Murat; he
has some lawyer friends and they'll take care of you." As
she speaks, I remember what I saw Murat doing in the
BMW. I forget all about myself and start feeling sorry
for Sevgi *Hanım*. They gather up our identity cards and
take off, leaving two officers behind to keep watch at
the entrance. I'm in less pain now, thanks to the IV and
the painkillers. They've bandaged my nose; I can feel
swelling around my eyes. I scraped the skin off my knees
when I fell and they sting like hell.

A few hours later the chief and his men come back
and take nine patients into custody, including me. Sevgi

Hanım tries to stop them, but it's no use. I get a window seat in the police van, and off we go. The guy driving the Audi Q7 next to us is clearly living off Daddy's money. He has the music turned up full blast and is tapping along on the steering wheel. He's probably studying at a private university. By next year he'll grow tired of the SUV and ask for a Mercedes CLX, and Daddy will probably get it for him, too. But, hey, the guy deserves it; after all, he isn't from *our* neighborhood.

The light just turned green.

I spend a hellish night alone in a cell at the station. Even though I'm dead tired, I hardly get a wink of sleep. In the morning they inform me that my lawyer has arrived. Murat *Bey*'s sent him. I tell him everything.

"All right," he says. "Don't worry, we'll do whatever we can. I'll try to keep you out of prison while we await trial."

The lawyer is married and has never in his life set foot in our neighborhood. He obviously drives a Volvo S70.

"What do you mean, trial? I've done nothing wrong."

"Of course you haven't, but the thing is, your photo is on the front page of all the papers," he says, taking a newspaper out of his leather briefcase. The headline reads VANDALS! and beneath it is a photo of me sitting in the middle of the road, my face covered in blood.

"But I didn't do anything!" I say. By now I'm starting to get scared. The lawyer reminds me of my right to remain silent and advises me to keep quiet at the police station but to tell the public prosecutor everything. He says we'll talk more if I'm detained, then shakes my hand and turns to leave. "Please let my mother know I'm okay!" I call out after him. He lifts his hand as if to say "All right." A policewoman takes me by the arm and leads me back to my cell. She's from our neighborhood; maybe her mother cleaned houses to put her through school, too. She's not married yet and right now she can only dream of owning a car.

Two days later they take us out of our cells. They tell us, "You're due in court." There are four other women besides me. I sit by the window in the police van. It fills up and off we go. As we make our way from Ulus to Sıhhiye, I find myself staring at the woman behind the wheel of the white Ford Focus right next to us. Definitely a rep for some pharmaceutical company. Well dressed, with a miniskirt and sunglasses that scream "I come from a different part of town!" It's a company car. This woman's single, too. She looks happy, but if you ask me, it's a mask to hide the drama going on underneath. She knows that happiness, like the car she's driving, doesn't belong to her; it's all company property, on temporary loan.

The light just turned green.

The public prosecutor asks short questions and I give short answers. He's young and still has a whiff of poverty about him. I figure he's married, probably owns a secondhand Nissan Almera. He's always hated being poor and now wants to speed away from it all, as fast as he can. He looks me in the face only once. My lawyer says, "There's no cause for detention," or something like that. The prosecutor tells us to wait outside. We wait in the hall for a good four or five hours. Once everyone has had their turn, they separate me and fifteen or twenty others and tell us the prosecutor has asked that we be kept in custody until our trial.

"Custody? What do you mean, custody?"

The lawyer tries to console me. A short while later, we're standing before a judge; he asks me the same questions and I give the same answers. The judge is married; he's forgotten how it feels to be poor and probably drives a new Škoda Superb, a black one with leather seats.

We speed through the darkness toward Sincan Prison. They won't let me sit next to the window in the police van, so I spend the entire trip sulking. The only sound comes from the police walkie-talkies. The women guards at the prison entrance tell us to take off our clothes so that they can search us. They're all from our side of the tracks, and they know they'll always be down on their luck. They can't even begin to imagine owning a car. We aren't the reason they're poor, but they still treat us like we are.

I've been in prison for six months now. I share a cell

with seven others, all from our neighborhood—feisty women who know a thing or two, if you catch my drift. My trial's in two months. My mother comes to see me every week during visiting hours. She's started cleaning houses again and says Sevgi *Hanım* sends her best. My mother cried on her first few visits, but she's holding up better now. It was my birthday last week. My friends made me a car-shaped cake out of cookies; we had a good laugh over that.

I am my father's daughter. The daughter of a man whose Mustang dreams were crushed beneath a rusty old city bus. A working woman who wound up in prison. I've never taken part in a demonstration, not once in my whole life. Being in here, I've come to see our neighborhood in a completely different light. And while I may not be in prison much longer, these six months have been enough for me to get to know myself. And there's an important lesson I've learned in here: If you walk with courage and determination, sometimes you can move faster than a car.

My name is Nazan the Cleaning Lady—look out, Ankara, here I come!

IT'S NOT WHAT YOU THINK

slipped the noose around my neck and gave the stool
a swift kick out from underneath me. As it tumbled
across the floor, I stared expectantly at the ceiling, lost in
thought, waiting for my life to flash before my eyes like
a reel of film. A good ten minutes passed and nothing
happened. Instead, each frame was filled with her smiling
face. My life—made up of her and her alone, those same
images running through my mind over and over again—
was about to come to an end. Or at least it would have
if I hadn't been flat on the floor. It turns out you can't

hang yourself lying down. On discovering this, I was
filled with a sudden desire to live. Having performed my
suicide attempt for the day, I stood up, removed the noose
from around my neck, and went into the kitchen to fry
myself three eggs for breakfast. Then I shaved, dressed,
and headed out of the house.

In the elevator I ran into Kadir, a retired mafia boss.
"Good morning Kadir *Amca*," I said politely, referring to
him as "uncle."

"And good morning to you, Musti," he said. "How's it
going?"

"Just fine, *amca*, I guess . . ." I mumbled. I actually
felt like saying, "You know what, Kadir *Amca*? I just
tried to kill myself." I longed for him to console me,
pat me on the head, show me some affection, a shred of
compassion. But instead I held my tongue and looked at
him like someone who had just tried to take his own life.
I wanted him to pick up on it himself. He didn't, and I
was devastated.

After stepping out of the elevator, he turned back
around and asked, "Something the matter with your eyes,
son?"

"No, *amca*, not really." I could barely hold back the
tears.

"Then why the hell are you wearing sunglasses in
the elevator, you idiot?" His response left me shattered,
like a watermelon that's fallen off a donkey, as the saying

goes. Except I felt more like the damn donkey than the watermelon.

I drifted through the streets, reminding myself that I had a good reason for not going to work today: I'm unemployed. I've been out of a job for two months now. And by job I mean pizza delivery. I used to deliver pizzas. Well, I did for one day, to be exact. The moped they gave me was stolen on my first day and so they told me not to come back. I'd never had a job before. My dad, bless him, sent me money each month. But when I started working for the pizza place, I told him to stop sending me the money. I didn't need it anymore. I was too ashamed to call him up the next day and tell him I'd been fired. My dad still thinks I'm a pizza delivery boy. Or, rather, he thinks I opened my own pizza place.

When he called last week, he said, "Son, I've been meaning to ask you: What is pizza, anyway?" He was up in the hills in Karlıova and the connection was terrible. In between the static I told him, "It's a kind of siding material."

"That's nice," he replied, before the line cut out. He called back a little later. "What's siding?" he asked. I didn't respond. And then the line went dead again.

I wandered along until I found myself in front of Berna's place. Berna wouldn't be at home at that time of day. She works at a bank, or for a bank, whichever it is. I met her at a stand in front of a supermarket.

"Can we interest you in a credit card, sir?" she asked. I told her no. She insisted, but again I declined. "All you need to do is let me photocopy your ID and we'll take care of the rest." I couldn't bear to let her down a third time, so I agreed to it.

"Great!" she said and signed me up quick as a flash.

The badge on her chest read BERNA, that's how I know her name. She knows mine, too, because she glanced at my ID while photocopying it. It's been seven months, but I'm sure she hasn't forgotten me. She gave me such a pretty smile. I went back to see her again the next day, followed her all the way home that time, but she didn't notice me. When she didn't show up outside the supermarket for the next few days, I went into the bank and asked where she was. They told me to take a number and wait my turn. When it was my turn, I repeated my question. They told me not to come back. And so I never did see Berna ever again. I waited by her house day and night, but I didn't get a single glimpse. Her smile is with me still.

My dad thinks I'm studying civil engineering here in Istanbul. It's been four years, so it's about time for me to graduate. But since I never finished high school, they wouldn't let me take the university entrance exam. Last year, my dad called to ask my advice about how to replace the earthen roof on our house.

"We haven't reached that chapter yet," I told him.

When Berna asked me my occupation, I said I was a civil engineer. I still carry that credit card with me. It was canceled when I failed to pay the first bill. I couldn't bear to throw it away, so I had it laminated and put it in my wallet. The repo men came to seize my belongings last month.

"Are you Mustafa *Bey*?" they asked.

"How can I help you?" I replied. They took everything I owned and left. If only I'd been able to find Berna, I would have explained to her why I didn't pay the bill. I'm so embarrassed I let the girl down.

The truth is, I'm not the kind of person you think I am. Before Berna, there was Nergis. She was the woman I loved, or at least wanted to love. She was Gıyasettin *Bey*'s daughter, and they lived in the apartment building across from mine. We once passed each other in the street and she gave me the prettiest smile. She was studying at the university, and I went there one day to visit her. I sat out front, waiting for her to finish a class. I thought about what I would say when I saw her. "Tell me, Nergis, in what way shall I love you?"

Shall I be your psycho stalker, carving your name across my chest with a razor blade? I'll break the hand of every man whose hand you shake—you who have not once deigned to hold mine. I'll be here every day, waiting for you outside these gates. I'll grab you by the arm and say, "Come, let's go somewhere, just the two of us." I'll smash my head into the face of anyone who tries to come between us. The more you tell me to leave you alone, the more I'll make your life a living hell. I'll camp out in front of your house late into the night. You'll peer out the window, shivering with fear but also shimmering with pride. You'll report me to the police. They'll take me to the station. With every blow I receive, I'll call out your name. Each blow will bring me closer to you. If *I* can't have you, Nergis, no one can; you belong either to me or to the deep dark earth. Life itself will become your prison; you'll lose all will to live. Then one day you'll tell me, sobbing, "Please, just leave me alone, I don't love you, I can't, I'm afraid of you. You're ruining my life, can't you see?" It's only then that I'll finally grasp the bitter truth. With a razor blade I'll carve my love into my wrists. I'll leave behind a letter, and you'll drown in your tears when you read it. Only then will you understand just how much I loved you. You'll come to my grave bearing a bouquet of wildflowers. And on my headstone it will say: IS IT ME YOU'VE COME TO SEE, NERGIS?

Tell me, Nergis, in what way shall I love you?

If you like, we can leave the university each day hand in hand. We'll be inseparable, like a pair of doves. Everyone will envy us. In the face of our love, all other couples will quarrel and break up. I'll call you "sweetheart" and you'll call me "darling." Two souls fused as one, we'll move in together, finally ending the torture of having to sleep apart. Our walls will be decorated with the poems I've penned for you. Our every moment together will be straight out of a fairy tale. We'll never tire of gazing into each other's eyes, and the most intoxicating scent in the world will be that of your skin. We'll live our lives as if the country's entire population were comprised of just us two. Then one day you'll learn that the number is actually three. You'll find out I've been sending presents to a girl named Ceyda. When you first hear about it, you won't believe it; it couldn't possibly be true, I would never do such a thing. But then, finally, for one reason or another, you do believe it. You'll be devastated. You won't leave the house for weeks. You'll lose faith in everyone, in humanity itself. You'll be disgusted by the mere thought of me. As I make my swift descent into the cold waters of the Bosphorus, you'll read the letter I've left behind for you. And as you read it, you'll drown in your tears. You'll learn that Ceyda is my sister and only then will you understand just how much I loved you. You'll come to my grave bearing a bouquet of wildflowers. And on my headstone will be written: IS THAT YOU, NERGIS?

So tell me now, Nergis, just how shall I love you?

If you like, our love can rise from the sacred foundation of labor and hard-earned sweat. As we rush from one protest to the next, your sweat and mine will become one. As our dedication to the struggle grows

stronger, so shall our passion for each other. We'll march
hand in hand down the glorious path of revolution,
discovering each other anew every single day. Put to
the test in ruthless interrogations, our love will become
twice-tempered steel. We'll play our part in shaping a
future that champions the downtrodden. We'll forge love
through labor and freedom through resistance. Courage
and sacrifice will be the sole laws of our rebel lives. Then,
one day, you'll break under torture and tell them where
I'm hiding. One morning, before the sun's rays have even
struck the red star upon my forehead, they'll raid the
house and put a bullet through my skull. Then they'll
find the letter I've left for you. And you'll drown in your
tears as you read it and only then will you understand just
how much I loved you. You'll come to my grave bearing
a bouquet of wildflowers. And on my headstone will be
written: IS THAT YOU AGAIN, NERGIS?

I can love you, Nergis, just tell me how!

For instance, our humble relationship could be undone
by a single well-rolled joint. From then on, we'll know
that whenever things get us down, all we need to do
is light up. We'll embrace the bohemian life and that,
Nergis, will be our demise. We'll work as bartenders,
you and I, just to pay for our weed. We'll rail against
inequality and injustice, if only as an excuse to roll
another one. Every day we'll break a new taboo, stocking
up on free love as we go. We'll neither count the days

that pass nor dream about ways to spend the future. We'll savor each moment without measuring its worth in dollars. We'll curse not at the fact that in Alaçatı one measly *lahmacun* costs fifty lira, but that it finds a buyer at that price. Olympos, now that'll be our spot. Then one day, while home alone, I'll lose it, this time completely. "Screw this shitty life," I'll say, and head out for a drink. After downing my fourteenth beer, I'll start a fight. The bar's owner will end up stabbing me. And in my pocket they'll find a letter addressed to you. As you read it . . . but wait, you know this part already. On my headstone will be written: ARE YOU FOR REAL, NERGIS?

And while all these scenarios were passing through my mind, I saw Nergis walking toward me and felt my knees grow weak as she came closer. Fortunately, I was sitting, so I didn't fall down. As she walked past, she didn't look directly at me, but she did glance in my direction. Though I'm certain her eyes were searching for me, she didn't see me. Her smile is with me still.

I wasn't always like this, it's not at all what you think. Everything bad that's happened to me has happened because of my love for a woman called Semra.

Semra appeared before me on a narrow street in the old marketplace full of the smell of spices and textiles. The second she saw me, she froze on the spot. As did I. For a few moments we conversed only with our eyes. The noisy street seemed to fall away, as if everyone else had disappeared and it was just the two of us alone. She hadn't changed at all and was every bit as enchanting as she had been all those years ago. At first, we hesitated. We could have pretended not to have noticed each other, just kept on walking to avoid opening those old wounds. Perhaps then we would have felt only a faint ache, one that would have faded by the time we reached the end of the street, turning at most into a pained smile as we went our separate ways. But that's not what happened. Instead, we walked toward each other and stood face-to-face, right in front of the barrels of red chili paste. The smell of that paste made my nose burn and I felt my eyes water from the pain. I held back my tears, afraid that she might read them the wrong way. And perhaps it was the chili paste that made her eyes well up, too, turning their green into the color of honey.

Why is it, I wonder, that spicy foods make our eyes water? There must be a scientific explanation. If only I'd known it at that moment, I could have used it as a conversation starter. Instead, I had no idea what to say. It was as if all words had been erased from my mind. From within the din of the marketplace I heard her say hello. Actually, it was so noisy that I didn't hear it, I just read the word on her lips.

"Hello," I said back, adding, "It's almost too much to bear."

"Yes, it is," she responded, looking at the chili paste.

Sheets of awning had been tied up to protect the market stands from the elements. Yet a sliver of sunshine had managed to slip through a crack and find its way down to her light brown hair; it was here that this ray of light completed a journey that had lasted millions of years. Who could have known when it set out all that time ago that it would turn the rest of my life upside down? As if we hadn't split up two years earlier, as if we were there that day shopping together, my hand went, of its own accord, straight for her hair, to brush aside that ray of sunshine.

"Don't," she said, but her voice reached my ears too late. I had already gathered all of the sun from her hair. A hand gripped my wrist. Both of us turned to look at its owner.

"Don't," my beloved called out, at the other man this time. The busy marketplace was punctured by a wail of pain. I didn't see her lips, but the sound pierced my ears. My beloved threw herself upon my bloodied body. And then came another sound. Her hair covered my face, its brown stained red with blood. A drop of honey fell from her eyes and onto my lips. The smell of blood mixed with the scent of spices, and the bustle of the marketplace gave way to pandemonium. You might think me coldhearted from the way I'm telling you all this. But the truth is, I, too, surrendered my soul that day. When my beloved departed, she took my life with her. It was her sad expression that dealt the fatal blow. My grave rests in Semra's bloodshot eyes, hers beneath a tree in the village. Her smile is with me still.

Everything bad that's happened to us has happened because of love. And now I live with a bullet in my head, a gift from Semra's brother. My mind comes and goes, but most of the time, it just goes. Every pretty smile I see takes me back to Semra. I no longer have the strength to keep tabs on the lives squandered for the sake of a smile. So, please, don't look at me like that. It's not what you think.

GREETINGS TO THOSE DARK EYES

t was six a.m. when the alarm clock rang. Hüseyin turned it off and climbed down from the top bunk, using his foot to nudge his bunkmate, Cemal, awake. He and Cemal were childhood friends. They were from the same village and had gone to school together until the end of third grade. Hüseyin had dropped out after that while Cemal stayed on for an extra year. This was why, every so often, Cemal would treat Hüseyin like an uneducated fool.

The moment his feet touched the floor, Hüseyin remembered that there was something special about

that day. It marked the end of their fifteen months at
the construction site—week after week of twelve-hour
days that seemed to last a lifetime, and night after night
with barely a wink of sleep. It had been a year and a
half since they had left the village in the hope of finding
work. The first three months they spent in Istanbul,
scraping by as day laborers, until finally they had the
good fortune of landing a job on this site. At first, the
manager was reluctant to take them on at all, since they
were only sixteen years old. In the end, though, he saw
the advantage of hiring them: He'd be able to get away
with paying them lower wages and avoid social security
altogether. And so Hüseyin and Cemal became two of
the eight children working there. They weren't the only
illegal laborers. Of the sixty workers, only twenty-six
had social security; the rest had agreed to go without.
Being a child was hard enough as it was. Harder yet to be
a child laborer. But for Hüseyin, the hardest thing of all
was the ache he felt for Berfin, the girl he had left behind
in his village.

That morning they left the dormitory, with its
acrid smell of sweat, and headed to the canteen, where
they gulped down their lukewarm soup. But instead of
walking straight to the construction site, as they had
done every day for the past fifteen months, they made
their way to the accountant's office to collect all those
months' worth of wages that were owed to them. Here,

they joined a long line of despondent, exhausted workers. They would take their money and head back to Istanbul to look for more work.

Hüseyin's love for Berfin was as innocent as he was, and as precarious as his job. Since leaving the village, he had written her two secret love letters. Actually, he couldn't address the letters to Berfin herself, so he had sent them to his sister, Zeliha. She's a smart girl, that Zeliha, she'll be sure to let Berfin know, he had thought. Even though Berfin's name was nowhere to be found in the letters, Zeliha was bound to figure it out and tell Berfin how much he missed her. But there was no mention of him missing anyone in the letters, either. He had made sure to keep everything as vague as possible so that no one caught on. He had put all his faith in that one line at the end of each letter: "I send my greetings to those dark eyes." But then everyone in the village had dark eyes—none as dark as Berfin's though. In fact, he had asked Cemal to write the letters, Cemal being the educated man that he was. When both letters went unanswered, he regretted his own lack of education even more.

A commotion broke out at the front of the weary line, rousing Hüseyin from his gloomy thoughts. He and Cemal exchanged looks. The news traveled down the line in a series of whispers until eventually it reached them: the accountant was nowhere to be found. Everyone had an opinion, some prediction about what would happen next. These workers, who had been toiling day and night for fifteen months without a word of complaint, were now muttering among themselves, as though on the brink of revolt. The wait dragged on for what felt like months. Then their angry voices faded to a tense silence.

Cemal had also forgotten to include a return address in the letters. What's worse, he had forgotten to write Zeliha's full address on the envelopes. The lack of reply kept Hüseyin up at night. Despite slaving away for twelve hours every day, he couldn't fall asleep. One night, lying awake on his bunk, he had written "Berfin" on the ceiling in ballpoint pen. Even in the dark, her name was visible. And while plastering the walls at the construction site, he would use his trowel to write "Berfin" again and again, smoothing it back over each time. Seeing Hüseyin in this lovesick state drove Cemal crazy. He tried to console him, lift his spirits, but it was no good. Eventually, he resorted to swearing at Hüseyin, once even tried to beat some sense into him. But Hüseyin would simply ignore him and go on with his daydreams.

Hüseyin's thoughts returned to the village, to the conversations he'd had with Berfin when they met up in secret. She had made it through the fifth grade before being taken out of school. That was more than enough education for a girl. And besides, it would soon be time for her to marry. Being a child in a tiny village in Muş was hard enough as it was. Even harder to be a girl. Harder still to be a child bride. Berfin, though, was a wild rose who never bowed to pressure. She refused to let her family marry her off and would cause a fuss each time they tried. Besides, she was secretly in love with Hüseyin. But she also had her sights set higher. Much higher, in fact. She had hinted at this to Hüseyin himself, had even spoken of leaving the village. It wasn't for nothing that his love was so intense, so consuming, and yet so hopeless. Hüseyin hadn't shared this with anyone, not even Cemal.

The foreman emerged from the site office, causing a stir down the line. He walked up to the men and calmly declared, "You can collect all your wages from headquarters in Istanbul." His words were met first with stunned silence, then with a rumble of dissatisfaction. The foreman turned to leave but stopped.

"The bus leaves in ten," he announced. "Any questions?" Again the workers responded with silence, then bowed their heads and fell out of line, dragging their feet toward the rusty old minibus that would take them to the city. A feeling of unease, and a profound sense of sorrow, took root in Hüseyin's heart.

If there was one other person in the world who thought of Berfin with the same sorrow, the same intense longing as Hüseyin, it was Berfin's mother. Two weeks after Hüseyin had left the village, Berfin disappeared. "My darling girl, don't let anyone harm you, not even a single eyelash. Be strong," she silently implored when her daughter failed to return home. And since that day, during morning prayers, she would turn her eyes to the heavens and pray for her wayward daughter, for her Berfin.

As the workers' minibus rolled slowly through the mud, Hüseyin turned to take one last look out the rear window at the finished building, the one they had built. A sign now hung above the entrance: EDIRNE F-TYPE HIGH-SECURITY PRISON. Cemal, too, turned and saw the same thing. Their eyes met. And then, as though caught red-handed, they averted their gaze in shame. The rusty old minibus left the work site for the highway, gathering speed, whisking the workers, registered and unregistered, young and old alike, away from their dreary pasts. As they sped along toward an uncertain future, Cemal rained down silent curses on Hüseyin and that damn sign, while Hüseyin sent his silent greetings to those dark eyes.

A LETTER TO THE PRISON
LETTER-READING COMMITTEE

Dear Committee,

I'm writing you this letter from a high-security prison
cell. "Why?" you might ask. Well, because I'm in prison,
if you must know. So now you're probably thinking, Yes,
we're fully aware of that. The question is: Why on earth
are you writing to *us*? We're going blind from reading all
your letters as it is. And that's exactly why I'm writing to
you. For pity's sake, what kind of career have you people
chosen for yourselves? You sit around all day reading

letters written by a bunch of strangers. What sort of life is
that? And to think they even pay you for it. (Indeed, they
do—the grand sum of 2,060 lira a month!) But that's not
the point here. To be honest, I'm not quite sure what the
point is. (Now, these last sentences have been "borrowed"
from an İlhami Algör story; I hope that won't be cause
for you to redact them.)

But I digress, so let me cut to the chase. I keep getting
requests from people on the outside (at least they *think*
they're on the outside) for just one more story. I've told
them it's best if I keep my correspondence brief from now
on, that the members of the letter-reading committee are
already at their wit's end. The poor things are working
their fingers to the bone because of me, and for what?
Besides, I tell them, it's not as if I'm a real writer or
anything. But, of course, when you grow up in a house
like mine, with a musician for a mother and a wordsmith
for a father, you can't help but pick up a thing or two.

Let me explain: As children, we woke each morning
to the sound of our mother playing the piano. Our house
had two rooms. We children all slept together in one of
them, the same room where our mother kept her piano.
Every morning, without fail, she'd sit down and bang
away at the keys, bless her heart. Believe me, the sound
still rings in my ears to this day. When we were a bit
older, she said to me, "Son, are you an idiot? What piano?
It's a sewing machine, for God's sake! I use it to make

some money on the side." But to our ears it was music, and that's what matters, right?

Dearest committee members, you might very well have children of your own—may God protect them—so let me give you a word of advice: If you want them to have a musical ear, don't bother with songs. Just make sure they're exposed to rhythm. Even the great virtuoso Arif Sağ owes his talent in large part to the rhythmic clapping of the water mill in the village where he grew up.

And then there's my father. He had a real way with words; they flowed from his mouth like verse. It was only when we were older that we realized it wasn't poetry but profanity. He was—and still is—a man with a great sense of humor and an utterly foul mouth. But you know how it is, swearing just suits some people and doesn't come across as rude. That's how my father is: when he swears, it's like poetry. One day, a friend of his from work stopped by and took offense when my father failed to swear once the whole time.

"What's the matter, Tahir *Abi*?" he asked. "Have I done something wrong?"

"What the hell are you talking about, you damn fool!" my father replied.

His friend breathed a sigh of relief.

And so there you have it; such was my early cultural upbringing.

I went to primary school in Diyarbakır. I was a studious boy and did well at school, very well, in fact. But I wasn't top of the class. That honor went to Bahir. He earned the highest marks and I was second only to him. Always neat and tidy, well behaved, and with impeccable handwriting, he was the model child. I wasn't so bad myself, but never quite as good as he was. I was popular at school and had lots of friends. Bahir had only one, and that was me. His family had moved to Diyarbakır from another city, or at least that's how I remember it. Nobody could pick on him because I wouldn't let them. We had this little gang of troublemakers and I was the leader (the co-leadership system didn't yet exist back then, of course). It soon became clear to us, though, that our gang wasn't as tough as we thought. There were others much tougher than we were. But again I digress . . .

I don't remember all that much about Bahir. I do have one vivid memory though. After school one day, we were walking home together through the narrow streets, tired and hungry, when Bahir exclaimed, "Mmmm, *pastırma*! Do you smell it?"

"Smell what?"

"*Pastırma, pastırma,*" he said.

"What the hell is *pastırma*?"

"You know, *pastırma,* that meat thing."

"What meat thing?" I asked.

"You know, that spicy meat that comes in thin slices," he answered.

I laughed. "What the hell do you mean, *pastırma*? There's no such thing as *pastırma*, you idiot." I teased Bahir about it the entire way home. I have to hand it to him, he didn't get upset or angry in the slightest. I'd never even heard anyone use the word *pastırma*, let alone seen it. When I got home, I recounted the tale, between fits of laughter, to my mother (you remember, the pianist).

"There *is* such a thing as *pastırma*, son," she said to me. "It's a spicy meat that comes in thin slices." I froze midchuckle. Forgive me, Bahir, I never told you about that.

In my second month in prison, I woke one night with a start. It was four in the morning. In my dream, Bahir had been saying to me, "*Pastırma*, don't forget the *pastırma*." I could hardly believe it; I didn't know if I was awake or still dreaming. A full thirty-five years later, in this high-security prison cell, my childhood friend had appeared to me in a dream to remind me of something. He looked exactly as I remembered him. As I'm sure you all know, we prisoners draw up a weekly list for the cafeteria. That week, Abdullah Zeydan and I wanted to treat ourselves, so we'd decided to ask for *pastırma*. I got out of bed and went downstairs to check the list, which was pinned to the bulletin board. What do you know,

we'd forgotten to include the *pastırma*. I thanked Bahir
and added it.

That night, for the first and only time since I'd been in
prison, I was overcome by a deep sense of sorrow. Bahir
and I lost touch after primary school, so I only knew
him as a child. Then one day, about ten years ago, if my
memory serves me correctly, I was skimming through
the newspaper when I saw a headline that read STAFF
SUICIDE AT DICLE UNIVERSITY. Under the headline was a
small, blurry photo taken from an identity card. Without
bothering to read on, I continued flicking through the
paper. But something made me turn back. I couldn't
believe my eyes; surely it couldn't be Bahir. I tried to
convince myself that it was just someone with the same
name, but there was no doubt about it: It was him in the
photo. I promised myself I would find his family so that
I could offer my condolences. Though it weighed on my
mind for a long time, I never did manage to find them.
Instead it was Bahir who found me, years later, visiting
me in my prison cell in a dream. Forgive me, Bahir, and
may you rest in peace, my dear friend. You were always
top of the class, and in my heart you will always be
number one; I never had the chance to tell you that.

Dearest committee members, I'm not quite sure
how I got onto this, but there you have it. Like I said,
my friends kept asking me to write another story from
prison. I insisted that I couldn't, that it just wasn't fair to

you, the committee. I have the utmost respect for you as workers of the world and the last thing I want to do is add to your workload. I just thought you should know. I wish you all a good day and the greatest success in your careers.

Respectfully yours . . .

THE MERMAID

My name is Mina and I come from Hama, in Syria. We left our home two months ago. My mama held on to me the whole time and didn't let go. Sometimes we walked, other times we rode on crowded buses and dusty trucks. The roads were full of potholes that bounced us up and down. But my mama never let me go. On the bus, people were always talking. And some of them cried. I cried, too. They killed my papa in Hama. I don't know why. My mama cried a lot then. And I cried, too.

We were on the road for so long. Two children died and an old man as well. The men dug graves for them by the side of the road. The children's graves were tiny. Their mothers lay on top of the graves, crying and crying. When it was time to leave, they didn't want to come with us, but the men dragged them away, told them we had to get going.

We arrived at a place where the bus stopped. Everyone got a little excited. Some of the men told us that when it was dark, we'd go down to the beach and get on a boat. But they told my mama she couldn't come. She begged them. Then she took out three bracelets from inside her blouse and gave them to the men. Okay, they said, you can come.

There was no sea in our village. I'd never seen the sea before. Neither had my mama. It was dark when we got to the beach and so we didn't really get to see it this time, either. The men loaded us onto a boat. There were so many of us. My mama held on to me and didn't let go. The men said to hold on tight to the side of the boat; my mama held on to me even tighter. The boat kept rocking. It was pitch-black so I couldn't even see the sea. Salty water hit me in the face, made me throw up. The old women said prayers and so did my mama. She told me not to be scared. It won't be long now, she said, we'll be there soon. I wasn't scared. The salt got in our eyes, made them water. But I cried a bit, too. The sea's rough today, the men said. They were always shouting. Hold on tight, they yelled. And then our boat turned over.

There was no sea in our village, but we had a small stream. The fish in it swam very fast. Actually, it wasn't that small; it was quite big. There were trees over by the stream. Once, my papa made me a swing in one of them. And our house was right next to the stream, too. Mama once made me a doll from old socks, but I forgot it on the bus. Our house was so pretty.

We all fell into the sea. My mama held on to me tight. We didn't have a sea in our village, so none of us knew how to swim. Not even Mama. Me and Mama started to sink in the water. Then we bobbed up again. But that big group of men, they kept pushing us down with their feet and so we'd go back under. My mama never let me go; she held on to me very tight. The salt in the water made my throat burn. Mama held on to me, and in my head I said to her, Don't be scared. I wanted to cry, but only a little. Mama wasn't scared, either; she looked into my eyes the whole time. We never got out of the sea.

My name is Mina and I'm five years old. We left Hama two months ago. We never had the chance to see the sea from the outside. I've been at the bottom of the sea for a week. Now I'm a real mermaid and the big white sea is my mother. She's wrapped herself around me and she won't ever let me go. That's what mothers do, because all mothers love their little girls.

KEBAB HALABI

It seems I was mistaken, life is very long . . ."

Is there anything strange about any of this? I don't think so. It's just another day in the Middle East, a bomb or suicide vest going off somewhere, leaving in its wake dozens of broken bodies and a shattered marketplace in a poor neighborhood.

Number of dead: 68. Read it—sixty-eight.

In the explosion three days ago, it was forty-three. Maybe death really is a commonplace occurrence and we are the ones blowing it out of proportion. People die all the time, and in droves at that. This afternoon's bombing in Aleppo didn't seem to have quite the same effect on Australians, who, at that very moment, were meeting up for dinner in Sydney's restaurants. And in Toronto, Canadians rushing to work won't even know about it yet. They'll learn about it soon enough, but most won't bother to read beyond the headline; it's just another ordinary explosion, after all. Aleppo is the closest city to Hatay. So close, in fact, that if the people of Hatay were listening carefully, they could have heard the explosion with their own ears.

Hatay is famous for its mezes and for the variety of dishes it has to offer. Drawing from the many cultures that have left their mark on these ancient lands, Hatay cuisine has everything you could wish for and more. Throughout their history, the people of Hatay have taken note of each and every delicacy consumed by the local Arabs, Armenians, Assyrians, Turkmen, Kurds, Turks, Persians, and Greeks, just in case they might need them one day. And, of course, as it turned out, they need them every single day. Anyone who visits Hatay and leaves without savoring these delights is certainly missing out.

Sixty-eight lives lost.

The Arabs of Hatay have a specialty known as the Arab kebab, a true work of art. You really ought to try it at Hamdullah *Usta*'s place, a shabby workers' restaurant in the old bazaar. Hamdullah *Usta* himself is like a character from a novel: the quintessential small-time business owner. As his restaurant grew in popularity, it began to attract tourists, too. This must have made Hamdullah *Usta* a little uneasy, as one day, in an attempt to spruce things up, he went out and bought half a dozen plastic trees and placed them around the restaurant. It was Sadrettin, the barber from across the street, who had given him the idea.

"*Abi,* you need to update your look," he'd said. "The street's starting to draw tourists already. If everyone would smarten things up a little, I swear they'd be coming here in throngs."

This made perfect sense to Hamdullah *Usta,* and that's how the plastic trees ended up there. The food is the same as ever, but now you can eat it in a faux forest setting. The only problem is, the trees are obviously fake and made of the cheapest plastic. They're also caked in dust. And so they did create a new ambience, just not the one he intended. But never mind, the food's as good as ever.

Sixty-eight dead.

There's only one waiter in the restaurant and he's Hamdullah *Usta*'s nephew. He can serve all seven tables at once without breaking a sweat. He's been working there since he was a child—a full nineteen years now. Bereket is his name. He has two children; his wife died last year in a traffic accident. By traffic accident I don't mean she flipped her fancy sports car. The poor thing was hit by a public bus on the main street and died on the spot. The kind of cheap death reserved for second-rate citizens. Bereket is a dedicated employee who adores his *usta*. He works with the utmost enthusiasm and presents every dish with an artistic flourish. He revels in satisfied customers and delights in even the tiniest spark of pleasure in their eyes. Choose anything from the menu, you can't go wrong—but the meat is truly out of this world.

Sixty-eight bodies ripped to pieces.

It's surprisingly affordable, too. I went there with a couple of friends and we had a real feast; when the bill came, we thought there must have been a mistake, they'd charged us so little. What I found most astonishing though is how Hamdullah *Usta* manages to stay so calm all the time. No matter how busy the place gets, he remains unfazed—dishing up plates behind the counter and handing them over to Bereket without the slightest change in his expression. I once went to Hamdullah *Usta*'s three times in a single week and was met with the same scene each time.

Hamdullah *Usta*'s family hails from Aleppo. It was his grandfather who moved them to Hatay, where they've been now for more than sixty years. Everyone knows them; the restaurant has been in the family for generations. His uncles own fabric shops in Aleppo's old bazaar, and before the war, they would often visit one another. But when the war broke out, his relatives, like

so many others, fled to Hatay. Hamdullah *Usta* pitched a
tent in the garden of his two-story house and they moved
in, all forty-seven of them. Given the circumstances,
Hamdullah *Usta* was forced to plead with the downstairs
tenant to leave, and when he finally did, it gave them a
little more space.

Hamdullah *Usta* never married. When he was a boy,
his father used to take him to Aleppo, and there he met
his cousin Rukiye and fell madly in love. But when
Rukiye was married off at the age of sixteen, he turned
his back on the world, never to love anyone again. And
now Rukiye lives with her husband and two children in
a room on the ground floor of his house. Hamdullah *Usta*
races out of the house each morning to avoid bumping
into her. For what it's worth, Rukiye has feelings for
him as well, but it's too late to do anything about it
now. She's still so beautiful he can hardly bear to look
at her, and when he does, he can't get enough. And by
"look," I mean nothing more than the briefest of glances
when they happen to cross paths every few days or so.
Hamdullah *Usta* is constantly on edge, as though they
have hatched a secret plan together and might take off at
a moment's notice, leaving everyone and everything else
behind.

Sixty-eight dead!

And because of this, Hamdullah *Usta* keeps his time
at home to a minimum, sneaking into the house at night,

after everyone else is asleep, and slipping into bed. He's terrified that someone might be able to read his thoughts. He's so worried that the flames of his love for Rukiye, rekindled after all these years, might become apparent to others that he has ceased conversing with Bereket altogether, not that they ever talked much to begin with.

He wants no one to notice his burning desire, its object downstairs in the room below, but he also wishes for those fleeting glances to grow longer. Each night he stretches them out in his mind until they envelop his silent world and send him to sleep. Is it a source of torment or comfort, knowing that she, too, breathes the air of this crowded beehive? But there's no answer to this question, you see. As the saying goes, the ground can but accept what the sky bestows. . . . So here they are, all these years later, under the same roof. And try as you might, there's no silencing that bird of hope perched on your roof. It's easy enough to chase that loudmouth away during the daytime. But once you've climbed into bed, all alone, and closed your eyes, there's no way to shut it out. And sleep is no escape, either. In your dreams the bird becomes bolder, even more brazen. What's worse, you have to wake up to face another day. "I'll take my time getting ready this morning," Hamdullah *Usta* says to himself. "Perhaps then, just maybe, I'll catch a glimpse of her. . . . No! Don't even think about it."

The marketplace in Aleppo is like a scene from a movie, frozen in time, its stalls selling nothing but despair. Since the war began, there's no joy to be found there, no colors, no smells. It has the somber air of a hospital ward, a place visited only out of necessity, to buy or sell scraps of food.

Sixty-eight human bodies ripped to pieces, Rukiye's among them. Two days earlier, she and her husband had left the children in Hatay to collect a few more belongings from their house in Aleppo. They had gone to the market to buy some things for dinner. Did you know, Hatay is famous for its *künefe,* too?

"Allahu Akbar!" cried the marketplace killer before he blew himself up. As Rukiye's body was being torn apart in Aleppo, Hamdullah *Usta* was performing the *namaz* on his wooden prayer mat at the back of the restaurant in Hatay. "Allahu Akbar," he said as he bent down in prayer. At that very moment he felt a pain in his chest. "I must be getting old," he said, sighing.

It's the cheese that gives the *künefe* its flavor. And, of course, in Hatay they have their own special way of making it. When his customers order it, Hamdullah *Usta* has it brought over from Cemil *Usta*'s *künefe* shop next door. Hamdullah *Usta* makes a mean *künefe* himself but stopped selling it as soon as Cemil *Usta* set up shop. There was enough business to go around, so it didn't seem right to encroach on his neighbor's territory. Though if it's the very best *künefe* in Hatay you're after, you really ought to pay a visit to the Hatay *Künefecisi* in the Long Bazaar.

Sifting through all the body parts, Rukiye's husband was able to pick out a few pieces of his wife by the fabric of her dress that still stuck to them. Hamdullah *Usta* couldn't bring himself to go to the funeral or even visit her grave. The evening after she was buried, he locked the door of the restaurant and swallowed every pill he could find in the medicine cabinet, washing it all down with cough syrup. The restaurant was closed for three days in mourning.

Bereket runs the place now. Rukiye's husband, Cuma, works for him as a waiter. Rukiye's two children do the cleaning and can always be seen bustling about. If you ever find yourself in the area, do pay a visit to Bereket *Usta*'s restaurant: the Arab kebab is as delicious as ever.

And, after all, Hatay is one of the oldest cuisines in the world.

ASUMAN, LOOK WHAT YOU'VE DONE!

The shudder of the bus woke me. I was sitting a couple of rows behind the driver. It was two in the morning and most of the other passengers were asleep. We were trundling up a hill, right behind a truck. I closed my eyes, hoping to doze off again, and when I opened them again a few minutes later, we were still traveling at the same speed, a steady two meters behind that same truck. Other cars were flying past us, yet our driver seemed strangely content to sit back and enjoy the ride. I needed to find out why. Quietly, I crept up to the front.

"What are we still doing behind this truck, Captain?" I asked, speaking into his ear. "Is something the matter?"

He raised his eyes to look at me in the rearview mirror. "Not at all. We're just cruising along, taking in the view. You got a problem with that?" he replied.

"No, no, I was just wondering. I mean, all these cars are passing us by—"

"Make yourself comfortable," he said, nodding toward the fold-down steward's seat next to him.

I hesitated.

"You a student, son?" he asked.

"Yes, I'm studying law at Ankara University," I replied as I sat down.

"Nice. Good school."

"Yeah, I suppose," I said with a hint of pride.

"Look at that, son," said the driver with a nod. "You see that?"

I looked out the windshield. It was impossible *not* to see the massive truck right there in front of us.

"Look closely," he said. "What do you see?"

"What? What do you mean?"

"The woman!"

I looked again. Right there, on the back of the truck, were two pictures of a woman. Or, to be more precise, there were two identical images plastered across the back doors, mirroring each other, the sort you'd see on almost every truck on the road.

"What about her?" I asked.

"That's Asuman!" he replied.

"You mean her name is Asuman?"

"Yes," he said, sighing. "I know that woman. In fact, I know her very well."

I smiled. "You see those same pictures on the back of just about every truck."

"True," he said. "They've got all kinds of pictures, but they're not all Asuman."

"Maybe," I replied. "I never paid them much attention."

"Me neither. Not till I met Asuman, that is."

"Are you telling me that you actually know this woman?"

"We met in a bar in Istanbul. About six years ago."

"Are you serious? You must be joking."

He gave me a look, picked up his pack of cigarettes, and held it out to me. I hesitated.

"Go on, take one," he said.

And so I did. He took one, too, and hung it from the corner of his mouth. The middle of his mustache was stained from a lifetime of smoking. He lit his cigarette and passed me the lighter. He took a long drag and thick smoke billowed from his nostrils, filling the bus. After cracking open his window, he settled himself in his seat and prepared to tell me the story of Asuman. I sat back and tried to look interested. It wasn't as if I'd be getting back to sleep soon, anyway.

"When a job took me to Istanbul, I'd sometimes go out to a bar in the evening," he began. He inhaled deeply on his cigarette, his eyes still fixed on Asuman. "That's where I first saw her, onstage at a bar in Aksaray. My God, could she sing! And you won't believe it, but I'm telling you, it was love at first sight. Just like in the movies. I couldn't take my eyes off her. And I caught *her* eye, too. Anyway, I'll keep it short—I went up to her afterward and introduced myself. She told me her name was Asuman. And then she shook my hand. It was like someone had handed me a red-hot coal: My entire body burst into flames. I told myself, 'Fahri, man, you're in deep shit now.' Nobody knows you better than you know yourself, right? I felt my heart twinge. I said to her, 'Let's get out of here.' She told me to come back the next day, but I said I'd be on the road. She asked if I was a truck driver. 'Bus driver,' I replied. She asked where I was headed and I told her, Diyarbakır. 'Ah well,' she said, 'next time then, Captain.' I didn't want to come on too strong, so I left it at that. A week or so later, I got another job driving to Istanbul. I have no idea how I even got there—my head was in the clouds and my heart was ablaze."

He took another drag on his cigarette and exhaled a plume of smoke into which his entire head disappeared. Cleaning his ear with the pinkie of the same hand that held his cigarette, he continued with his story.

"So, anyway, I went back to that bar, and this time we left together, stopped at some late-night soup joint. And we hit it off—like a house on fire, I tell you. She'd taken quite a shine to me, too, and so there we were, talking and talking, pouring our hearts out to each other. I ended up staying at her place that night, but I had to head back to Diyarbakır the next afternoon. Anyway, to cut a long story short, things carried on like this for about a year. Whenever a job took me to Istanbul, I'd stay with her, till finally I asked her to come with me to Diyarbakır. 'I'll rent you an apartment and you can take it easy, you won't have to work anymore.' Those were my exact words."

"Come on, Captain," I interrupted. "This whole thing sounds like some sentimental Turkish melodrama if you ask me."

He shook his head gently and smiled. "Fine, I won't bother telling you the rest then."

"No, no, I'm sorry. I just meant that it sounds like the plot of a soap opera," I said.

"Well, let me tell you, son, that's *exactly* what it was like," he replied.

He picked up the handset next to him and called the steward. Sleepy-eyed, the man shuffled over. "Bring us two coffees and make them strong," the driver ordered. "And don't sleep on the job," he chided. "Go check on the passengers." Our coffees arrived straightaway.

"So anyway, son, I wrecked my own home for

Asuman, left the wife and all three kids. I rented an
apartment for her in Diyarbakır and we got an imam
to do what was necessary. A religious ceremony, if you
catch my drift. I didn't divorce the old wife, not officially,
and—with God as my witness—I still made sure she was
looked after, sent her money every month as a kind of
alimony. Anyway, I won't bore you with the details. In
the end it didn't work out: Asuman left me. One day I got
home and everything was gone, she'd cleared the whole
place out. The only thing she left was a note. It said, 'I've
taken the furniture as alimony. Don't try to find me.
Asuman.' That night I stayed in a hotel. In the morning
I bought a bunch of flowers and took them to the wife.
God knows, my old lady's not one to hold a grudge, I
thought to myself. And, besides, she knows how these
things go. She took the flowers and whacked me over the
head with them, cursing the day I was born. She did have
a point though. I thought she just needed some time and
that sooner or later she'd come around. But, boy, was I
wrong about that. She divorced me as quick as she could,
leaving me all alone again, like the fool that I was."

Eyes fixed on the back of the truck, he let out a deep
sigh.

"Asuman, look what you've done! You wrecked my
home, you ruined me. Asuman, Asuman, Asuman. . . .
So that's how it is, son, that's the story of Asuman."

Motioning again toward the truck, he continued, "She used to model every now and then. That there is a photo from one of her shoots. I even have the original. And whenever I see it on a truck I just pull in behind and tag along for as long as I can. Luckily there aren't many pictures of her out there, otherwise I swear I'd never get anywhere," he said. He turned to give me a bitter smile.

"Isn't driving like this a little dangerous, Captain?" I said. "You drifted off into your own world when you were telling that story, even closed your eyes sometimes."

"Don't you worry, son, I've got it all under control. But you know how it is—you always close your eyes when you dream of something. That way, no one sees your dreams. And when you close your eyes, you hide them even from yourself. Because the real you is actually the person in your dreams."

"What can I say, Captain, I'm speechless." (I wanted to add, "Your Asuman may as well have quoted Nietzsche: 'After you discovered me, it was no great feat to find me. The problem now is how to lose me,'" but I thought better of it.) "You're a bus driver, though, all these people's lives are in your hands. You really ought to be careful, God forbid something should happen."

"Of course," he replied. "That goes without saying, but sometimes I get to thinking—there are so many ways to die: you could burn, you could drown, you could fall; your death could be slow and painful or perfectly ordinary; you might die a hero or for no reason at all. And all that's true for living as well as dying. Strange, isn't it?" he mused.

"You're an odd man, Captain," I said. "And by odd I mean interesting."

I turned again to look at Asuman. She was lying on her side, gazing seductively at the camera, her elbow propped up on a cushion, her cheek resting on her hand, her face fully made-up. That Asuman, she's a piece of work, I thought. Turning back to the driver, I was met with a mischievous grin.

"You're studying to be a lawyer, are you?"

"That's the plan," I said.

"*Mashallah!* You are one bright spark," he replied sarcastically. "God help the man who hires you."

"What do you mean by that, Captain?"

"Look, son," he said, smiling. "You probably slept through it, but the bus broke down a while ago and we hitched ourselves to this truck in front of us. They're going to tow us to the top of Mount Gavur. Take a look out front and you'll see the towrope."

I didn't want to believe him. I leaned forward and looked out; sure enough, there was the rope. Asuman really was towing us along. I was embarrassed to have fallen for his tall tale. "Stop the bus, damn it," I wanted to say, "I'm getting off!" But there was nothing I could do; I had fallen for it hook, line, and sinker. The driver had a smirk on his face, or so it seemed to me. He called the steward back over.

"Show the boy back to his seat," he said. "And give him some cologne, it'll help him come to his senses."

"Well done, you had me there, Captain," I mumbled as I returned to my seat. To make matters worse, the steward really did bring over the cologne and sprinkled a few drops onto my hands.

"You'll get over it, *abi*," he said, with a wide grin. I saw the driver looking at me in the rearview mirror, a smile still on his face.

Many years passed. But I recognized him the moment he stepped into my office: Captain Fahri. I ushered him in and ordered us tea. He was graying at the temples and his bushy mustache had gone completely yellow. He was thinner than before and stooped a little. He didn't recognize me, but that was no surprise; it had been such a long time since we'd last seen each other. Besides, he was in no state to recognize anybody; his son, a university student, had been arrested for taking part in a demonstration. For two months he'd been searching in vain for a lawyer willing to take the case. A friend of his had recommended me.

"All right," I said, "let me take a look at the file. Come

back again tomorrow and we'll talk." He stood and clasped my hand, his head bowed. I bowed mine, too, and then saw him out.

I took on his son's case; four months later he was released and then acquitted. Soon after, the two of them turned up at the office to thank me, bearing flowers and chocolate.

"Why wouldn't you let me pay you?" he asked.

"You don't remember me, do you, Fahri *Abi*?" I said.

He fixed his eyes on me intently, trying to place me. "Beg your pardon," he said. "Where should I know you from?"

"From Asuman."

He froze, staring at me in astonishment. The smile that spread across his face soon turned to laughter, and he stood up and hugged me.

"My, my! But remember what I said to you that day?"

"What was that, Fahri *Abi*?"

"Didn't I say that you'd be a great man, that anyone who hired you should count his lucky stars? Didn't I?"

"Of course you did, Fahri *Abi,* of course you did."

Fahri was delighted and from that moment on we were like two long-lost friends reunited at last. "The two of us go back a long way," he told his son, before launching into the tale of the bus journey, fortunately skipping over the embarrassing details. The pair stood up and I saw them to the door. Just as they were leaving, I called out to him, "Fahri *Abi*."

"Yes, son?"

I took a bottle of cologne from the secretary's desk and sprinkled a few drops into his outstretched hands.

"You'll get over it, *abi*!" I said.

He gave me a warm smile.

"I hear you, son," he said. "Now it's my turn to repay the favor. The question is, how?" And with a shake of his head, he closed the door.

SETTLING SCORES

t was 1981. I was eight, my brother, Nurettin, was nine. That was a tough year for us both. A brutal military coup had taken place just a few months earlier. We weren't aware of what that meant yet. But, anyway, Mother, this has nothing to do with what I want to say to you.

We'd run out of sugar at home. We usually bought it by the kilo from the store downstairs, but buying it like that was more expensive. So on that day you sent us out to the wholesaler a kilometer from our house to buy five kilos. At the store five kilos of sugar came to

113

300 lira; wholesale it was 250. Nurettin and I went and bought the sugar with the 250 lira you'd given us. As I was the smaller one, it was my brother who carried the bag of sugar. He'd barely made it a few steps before he got tired and put it down. We took a break and then we each picked up one end of the bag and started carrying it together. After a few steps, exhausted, we placed it back down again. That bag of sugar was just too heavy for us. We gave in and walked over to the horse and cart parked at the side of the road. My brother told the driver where we lived and asked how much it would cost to take us there. The driver gave us a strange look and glanced over at the bag of sugar. "Fifty lira," he said. We'd never even heard of such a thing as haggling, so we immediately agreed. We slung the bag of sugar onto the cart and then climbed on ourselves. The whole way home, we sat with our legs dangling over the side. Our apartment was on the fifth floor and the driver carried the bag of sugar up to our front door. He didn't have much of a choice: We didn't have any money on us, so he had to come up if he wanted to get paid.

When you answered the door, Mother, we told you what had happened. At first you thought it was a joke. You soon realized it wasn't and went inside to get the money to pay the driver. We'd ended up spending just as much buying the sugar from the wholesaler as we would have if we'd bought it from the corner shop downstairs.

But what you didn't realize at the time was that my brother and I were staunchly opposed to the monopolization of capital. We were advocates for the redistribution of wealth at a grassroots level. Rather than giving the entire 300 lira to the shopkeeper, we'd given 250 to the wholesaler and 50 to the driver. This was the first real action of our budding political movement. But you weren't convinced and so the movement fell apart before it could even get going. It's your fault that Turkey became a free market economy, and look where that got us. What a huge burden that must be for you to live with—huge!

And then there was the time you dished up some homemade yogurt into a tiffin box and told us to take it to our *Hadji* Grandpa's. My brother and I took our time, dawdling our way through all four neighborhoods. It was afternoon by the time we got there and we were exhausted.

"You must be hungry," our *Hadji* Grandma said and gave us some bread to eat, along with the yogurt we'd brought. We devoured the whole lot. Grandma washed out the tiffin box and gave it back to us; we took it and headed home.

"What kept you boys so long?" you asked us. We explained we were late because we'd had lunch at Grandma's. You asked what we'd eaten and we told you we'd had yogurt.

"Please tell me it wasn't the yogurt you've just taken them," you said in disbelief.

"Of course it was," we replied, as though it were the most natural thing in the world. For years after, you'd repeat this story to anyone who'd listen and have a good laugh at our expense. But I never saw anything unusual in what we'd done. Even if I couldn't quite find a way to explain our actions, it always seemed perfectly logical to me. I'd put plenty of thought into this before, but it wasn't until prison that I finally understood it. You sent Grandma and Grandpa the yogurt not because they needed it, but because you wanted to make them happy. And we had achieved that the moment we handed it to them. But what made them even happier was watching their darling grandsons wolf down that very same yogurt. Your reason for sending the yogurt was to create a single moment of happiness, but we doubled it. So, you see, it's not fair! For the last thirty-six years you've all been laughing at us for no good reason, you big bullies!

That was also the year we got into the prayer-cap business. You'd sit at home and crochet prayer caps out of acrylic yarn, and Nurettin and I would go out and sell them. It's true that business might not have been as brisk as we'd hoped, but there was a slump in the global prayer-cap market that year. You always blamed our pitiful sales on the marketing department, though. We, on the other hand, never once thought to question the flaws in the production process. The fashion that season was for finely woven, pastel-colored prayer caps. That was true at least for the *hadji* uncles' segment of the market. You, though, insisted on crocheting thick caps in burgundy, khaki, black, and red. Really, Mother: When have you ever seen green and red prayer caps? But you kept on making them, anyway. We should have set up shop outside the Diyarbakır football stadium—who wouldn't want a prayer cap in their team's colors? Instead we were out there trying to peddle our wares in front of the Grand Mosque! We ended up selling most of the caps to *Hadji* Grandpa. Whenever business was slow, we'd head over to his store, where we'd be treated to wafer biscuits, and sell a couple of caps to boot. For the record, we sold at least twenty to your own father. And may I remind you, you only made twenty-five in total.

You'll also remember the time our father came home from work for lunch. This wasn't something he did very often; it just so happened that he fancied having lunch at home that day. You were in a rush to set the table and sent us down to buy bread at the store. For some reason, whenever you said "store," only one place came to mind: Grandpa's. Once again, we took our time getting there, had our wafer biscuits, and then ambled back home. A good three hours had passed by the time we got back.

"Where've you boys been?" you cried, obviously worried.

"We went to Grandpa's," we replied. When you asked us where the bread was, I turned and looked at my brother. The look was meant to say, "*He's* the purchasing manager for bread, what are you asking *me* for?" But you weren't falling for it. Our father had his lunch without any bread that day. Now I'll admit, I still haven't found a rational explanation for this one. So let's just move on. After all, 1981 was a tough year. But tough times eventually come to an end, Mother, they always do. I kiss your hands in gratitude, and the hands of mothers everywhere.

AS LONELY AS HISTORY

My father and I never spoke much. They say that fathers are especially fond of their daughters, but I never got that impression from mine. All my life I'd known him to be rather withdrawn. Not just with me, but with everyone. I had never once seen him and my mother argue, but neither did I believe them to be bound by any deep passion for each other. My mother accepted him the way he was, and settled for the uneventful life they led. I can remember only a handful of joyful moments, with the two of them laughing and talking merrily.

We owned a large rose garden in Isparta, and my father sold roses for a living. He and my mother spent all their time harvesting and then selling them. My father had barely finished middle school and my mother never learned to read and write at all. Before I was born they'd had a child, who died at just two months old, and no more children followed me. I used to lend a hand in the rose garden when I was little, but I never much cared for the rose business myself. I wanted to go to university and my father encouraged me.

I passed the entrance exam and went to Istanbul to study architecture. Except for the occasional brief visit during the summer, I hardly ever returned to Isparta. When my mother passed away five years ago, I went back to spend a week with my father. I didn't want him to be alone. We barely had a real conversation the entire week. My father kept his grief to himself. Still, I could sense the void my mother's passing had left in him.

My mother and I were closer. We would speak on the phone several times each week, and shared almost everything. Though it took a lot of persuading, she came to visit me twice in Istanbul and the two of us saw all the sights together. I never bothered to invite my father—he wouldn't have come, anyway. When my mother died suddenly, I felt as if I'd been orphaned. I had lost my mother and didn't even feel as though I had a father. I certainly didn't expect him to fill my mother's shoes. And I don't think he had any expectations of me. I knew that he loved me, we'd just never been close enough for him to show it, I suppose. I can't recall a single instance when he ever treated me badly or even raised his voice. He was a calm, silent person: a good man.

After our week together, I told my father that I needed to return to Istanbul.

"Of course, sweetheart, you should get back to your own life," he replied. "Don't you worry about me." It was the first time I'd ever heard him speak with such emotion in his voice.

"Why don't you come, too?" I suggested. "Come stay with me for a while, it would be a nice change for you."

I surprised even myself with the sincerity of my invitation, but my father seemed to take it as the most natural thing in the world. "Thanks, sweetheart, but I'm fine right here for now. It's almost time for the harvest. Once that's over, I'll think about what comes next."

We said our goodbyes and I left.

Work had really piled up while I was away, and when I got back to Istanbul, I threw myself into my daily routine. It felt good to concentrate on my job. I owned an architecture firm together with my partner, Fırat, and our business grew quickly. It wasn't long before we were working on projects beyond our wildest expectations.

All over Istanbul, neighborhoods had been earmarked for urban redevelopment, and we'd managed to get in on the action.

Fırat and I had been friends since university. In our final year we'd starting dating, and after graduation we set up the architecture firm. I'd introduced him to my mother when she came to visit me in Istanbul. After they'd gotten to know each other a little she said to me, "This one's a keeper, darling; don't let him get away." I followed my mother's advice and married him. But not until about a year after she died. I called my father to tell him the news.

"That's great, sweetheart," he said. "I'm so happy for you." We celebrated with a simple ceremony among close friends. My father didn't come, but he did call that evening to congratulate us both.

About a month after the wedding, my father called to tell me he'd sold his plot of land.

"I'm moving to a small place in Finike, sweetheart," he said. "I'll let you know the address. Don't you worry about me."

I wished him the best and told him to call me if he needed anything. A couple of weeks later he sent a message with his new address in a fishing village in Finike, saying that he was settled and that we were welcome to stay with him anytime.

I promised we'd pay him a visit and told him to take

care of himself. I made sure to call at least once a month to ask how he was. Most of the time he replied that he was perfectly content and enjoying his retirement.

Fırat and I made good partners, and our marriage was as successful as our business. We worked six days a week and usually spent our Sundays lounging around the house. On Saturday evenings we'd meet up with friends in Beyoğlu and have a few drinks, then go to the movies or the theater and wind down from the busy week. Fırat was a real literature buff. I liked to read, too, but not as much as he did. He kept up with all the new titles, followed all the reviews, and then on the weekends he would hit the bookstores, emerging each time with an armful of books. His passion soon rubbed off on me. When he read a novel he particularly liked, he'd always pass it on. I trusted his taste and was never disappointed. One day, he was lying in bed reading, as usual, and after turning the last page, he placed the book on his chest and stared at the ceiling, deep in thought.

"Incredible! This man really knows how to write," he said. "It's only his first novel, but it's so well crafted." He held the book out to me. "You have to read this, you'll love it."

The very title sounded profound: *As Lonely as History*. The author's name was Hasan Vefa Karadağlı. According to the biography on the back jacket, he was a retired mechanical engineer. There was little other information about him, just enough to work out that he was older than he appeared in the photo. I turned the book over, had a quick flip through it, then placed it on the bedside table, telling Fırat I'd read it later.

In many of Istanbul's neighborhoods, buildings were being demolished at a furious pace, only to be replaced by high-rise luxury condos. For us, the money had started to pour in, especially from our projects in the Fikirtepe neighborhood, so much so that our lifestyle was completely transformed. We invested our savings wisely, buying properties due for redevelopment and then selling them on as soon as they were finished. This made us some extra income on the side, in addition to what we were earning at the firm. Between the unrelenting pace at work and our constant desire to earn more, we had turned into machines. We were so busy making money that we had no time to spend it. Apart from those NGOs campaigning against the redevelopment projects, our lives were for the most part worry-free. As for whether or not I was happy, well, I barely had time to give it any thought. We were working hard, making decent money, and living the good life. As for our relationship, other than not seeing much of each other, Fırat and I didn't have any problems to speak of.

Work kept me so busy that I was only ever able to squeeze in a few pages of reading at night before bed. It was a week before I got around to reading *As Lonely as History,* and it had me hooked from the first page. I couldn't put it down. I was almost halfway through before I finally had to surrender to sleep. The following day I couldn't get the book out of my head and left work early to get home and pick up where I'd left off. Fırat called from the construction site to say he was heading to the office that evening and would be working late. I took the opportunity to immerse myself in it once more. By the time Fırat walked in, having unlocked the door quietly so as not to wake me, I had reached the last page. Seeing me in the living room, he asked what I was still doing up. I didn't want to break my concentration, so without lifting my head, I shushed him. For several minutes he stood there watching me, eagerly waiting for me to finish. Once I had, I turned to him.

"What an extraordinary book! You weren't exaggerating."

"See? It got to me, too. It really captures what it means to be lonely in a crowd," Fırat replied, drawing closer to me. "Sometimes I get to thinking, Nermin, we work so hard, but what exactly do we get out of it other than money? It only makes me feel alone and that scares me sometimes. Think about it: Climbing the social ladder is like heading off into outer space. The higher you get, the lonelier it becomes. You grow further and further apart from others, and from society itself, until you find yourself in a vacuum with nothing for company but your solitude. And the saddest part is that you run yourself ragged day and night trying to get there. It's as if we're these pathetic creatures who have made a conscious decision to abandon a place so full of life and make our way toward some barren wilderness instead." Fırat spoke these words almost as if to himself.

"You know what, you're right," I replied. "It's about time we had a change in perspective. It's almost like this novel was written for us. If we want to get our lives on track, we'll need to look beyond ourselves and reconsider our priorities."

Fırat looked me in the eyes. "Nermin, I have an idea: Let's take a long vacation, just the two of us. We can leave in the morning. It'll give us a chance to think this all over, to really talk it through. And we can get some rest, too. What do you say?"

I paused for a moment. "We can't leave tomorrow, not when things are so busy, it would be total chaos," I explained, trying to let him down gently.

As we placed our suitcases in the trunk early the next morning, neither of us could quite believe what we were doing. As soon as we set off, we planned the route our trip would take: We would travel down the Aegean coast until we reached Finike, where we'd pay a quick visit to my father before heading back. I called to tell him we were on our way and that we'd be with him in about ten days.

"Drive carefully now, sweetheart," he replied. "Have a safe trip."

As Fırat and I slowly made our way down the Aegean coast, we talked about our past and about our future, too. We discussed the state of the country, and of the world in general, and all the horrors carried out in the name of progress: cultural decay, environmental disasters, the growing individualism crippling human relationships, how the concept of love had been turned on its head. . . . We discussed it all. By the time we reached Finike, both of us felt refreshed; the trip had been like therapy for us.

My father had given us directions to his village, and we found it with little difficulty. It consisted of half a dozen shops and eateries, set in a grove of trees by the side of the road, and twenty or so houses that dotted the forest a little farther up the hill. When we pulled up in front of the village coffeehouse, my father was sitting outside at a wooden table with three elderly men who appeared to be locals. As soon as he spotted us he stood up and began walking toward the car, a broad smile on his face. He greeted us with an embrace. Then he took a step back and looked Fırat over. Even though we'd already been married for two years, it was the first time they'd met. Fırat had been a little nervous, but this warm welcome put him at ease. My father introduced us to his friends and then suggested the three of us head over to his house. The owner of the coffeehouse insisted on treating us to tea, but my father declined, joking, "I make better tea at home than anything you can brew here!" And with this he set off, telling us to follow him.

We passed by a fish restaurant with a front garden shaded by vines and full of flowers of all colors, and then a small village café, its tables beneath gazebos in yet another extraordinary garden. Beyond that was a stand selling handmade gifts and local produce, and finally we came to a garden resplendent with roses—we had arrived at my father's house. Standing in one corner of the huge garden was a small structure that looked more like a shed than a house. Under the arbor, two simple benches, topped with kilim-covered cushions, had been set up on either side of a large wooden table. The garden was filled with fruit trees and roses of every color. After so many years of cultivating roses, my father had clearly brought all his talents to bear here in this garden. We sat down on one of the wooden benches, and through the fruit trees we could glimpse the endless sea stretching out beyond the road. My father headed inside, saying he would be right back with some tea. Fırat and I looked at each other and then leaned back, taking in the stunning view and the tranquil setting. Other than the occasional car driving past on the road just down the hill, the only sounds to be heard were the waves crashing against the shore and the whirr of crickets falling softly against the faint whistle of a cool breeze. I thought of how enchanting this place was, this village where my father had chosen to spend his remaining years, and I have to admit, I was a little envious. Weary from the journey, we were tempted to curl up on the benches and take a nap. Before long, my father returned with a teapot in one hand and a tray of glasses in the other. The tea was every bit as delicious as he'd promised. We sat there talking for hours, about our work, what we'd been up to, and my father's new life in the village. It was clear he had made the right decision moving here after my mother's death; the gentle pace had done him good. He was a little more talkative than usual though still not an easy man to read, but I didn't think there was much there to read, anyway. I was happy to see him so at peace. Despite his insistence, we turned down his invitation to spend the night. We had to get to Antalya for an evening flight back home. We'd arranged for the car to be brought to Istanbul by a delivery service. Realizing it was no use trying to convince us to stay, my father conceded, adding, "Well, then, at least let me treat you to dinner before you go." Truth be told, all the fresh air had made us hungry, and we couldn't refuse.

Each of the places along the road, including the fish restaurant where we went, were owned by locals, all of whom my father had befriended. Sitting at one of the wooden tables in the restaurant's garden, we feasted on the delicious mezes, fresh fish, and homegrown salad. As we drank our tea, my father recounted anecdotes from his time in the village, his eyes gleaming with joy, until finally the time came to say our goodbyes and head home. The whole way back, Fırat spoke of nothing but how impressed he was with my father, what a delight he was to talk with, and how we should try to see him more often.

Returning to work the next day, we felt rejuvenated, as though we ourselves had embarked upon a brand-new life. Our lives would no longer consist only of work and money; we would rearrange our priorities and take a greater interest in the world around us. At least, that was what we resolved to do during our trip. Yet barely two weeks had passed before Fırat and I were back to our old routines, working harder than ever. And though we would never admit it to each other, we looked back on all that we'd discussed while away as a kind of confession, an attempt to purge ourselves of the sins of our success. The occasional daydream never hurt anybody, after all.

Very little changed over the next two years. With business booming, we eventually had to move to larger offices. Our team of twelve architects and engineers took care of the company's day-to-day business while Fırat and I pursued ever-bigger projects. We worked feverishly, fueled by a constant worry that should we stop working, even for a single day, we'd lose everything. Sometimes we wouldn't see each other for days on end. And at night we'd pass out from exhaustion, only to rise at the crack of dawn and dash off to the office or one of the construction sites. Yet the fortune we'd amassed was more than we could spend in ten lifetimes, let alone one. And neither I nor Fırat had any close relatives to share it with. Or, rather, we weren't close enough to any of them to think of ourselves as relatives. And we were so busy that the thought of children never even crossed our minds. We weren't unhappy, and we mistook this for happiness itself.

One typical Saturday evening, we were wandering around Beyoğlu when we saw a poster for Hasan Vefa Karadağlı's new novel, *It's Love That Stays with You,* in one of the bookstore windows. We rushed in and bought two copies, one for each of us. "I hope it's as good as the first," Fırat said. Not only had *As Lonely as History* been a bestseller in Turkey, but critics had loved it and it had won numerous awards and been translated into many languages.

We spent the following day at home reading. Both of us were so engrossed that it was evening before we even thought about food. When Fırat reminded me that we needed to eat, we hurriedly prepared a meal, which we ate as quickly as possible in order to get back to our books. The writing was so remarkable that we couldn't put them down; we read straight through and reached the end around midnight. When Fırat, book in hand, emerged from his office, he found me lying on the sofa in the living room, my tired eyes fixed on the ceiling. Karadağlı's first novel had prompted us to do some genuine soul searching. And although we had drifted from our resolutions for the most part, the book had reinvigorated us, opening our eyes to how unfulfilled we felt despite our great wealth. This second book, though, could as well have been about us. It spoke of how we always played by the rules of others, our lives carefully designed to meet the system's every whim, extinguishing our passion and plunging us into darkness. We sat up all night, talking about this and more: about our lives, our relationship, and the ghost of what was once our love, about the impasse in which we were trapped, about whether there was any going back, and if the fortune we had amassed in the bank would be enough to make up for the love we had lost. . . . It was hard for us both to admit that for a long time now, we had seen each other as nothing but business partners.

"It seems we're due for another vacation," Fırat concluded with a laugh.

"I hope you don't expect us to hit the road first thing in the morning like last time," I said.

"No, no. This time, we'll take a few days to plan ahead."

"All right, let's see," I replied. "But for now we've got to get to the office."

We each took a shower and had a quick breakfast, before dragging our tired bodies into work.

The office was bustling as usual. The novel still had my mind reeling, and this, combined with my lack of sleep, drained me of any motivation. I spent the morning wandering around aimlessly. Finally, toward noon, I gave in and curled up on the sofa in my air-conditioned office. I was startled awake by my phone ringing. I didn't know how long I'd been asleep, but I didn't feel at all rested. Fırat must have stopped by at some point, judging by the blanket covering me and the pillow beneath my head. Reluctantly, I reached out and picked up the phone from the coffee table; it was an unknown caller. I considered putting the phone on mute and going back to sleep, but the caller was insistent.

"Yes, hello?" I answered in a sleepy voice.

"Nermin, dear? Is that you?" It was the unfamiliar voice of an old man.

"Yes, it is. But I'm sorry, who is this?" I asked, curious.

"It's Selim, from Finike. Your father's friend, the fisherman."

"Oh, right, Selim *Amca,* of course," I replied. "I'm so sorry, I didn't recognize your voice." Now I was worried. Why would Selim *Amca* be calling me?

"I'm sorry to bother you, dear, but your father's not

doing so well, he's at the hospital in Finike. It's best if you come straightaway." As soon as the words were out of his mouth, I leaped off the couch.

"What's wrong with him, Selim *Amca*? Is it serious? Are you with him?" I asked, concerned.

"He's not doing so well, dear. It's best if you come, that's all I can say," he said before hanging up.

I could tell from his tone that it was serious, but I still didn't want to assume the worst. I pulled myself together and called Fırat, who was out at one of the construction sites. I quickly explained the situation and told him to meet me at the airport.

It was almost midnight by the time we reached the hospital. Selim *Amca* and the other villagers were waiting for us out front. The sight of them standing there told me everything we needed to know. For a moment I thought I might faint, but Fırat held me by the arm. They sat me down on a bench while offering me their condolences. It's true that my father and I had never had a conventional father-daughter relationship, but I never imagined his death would crush me in this way. Though we weren't particularly close and didn't see each other that often, he was my father, and now he was gone. There in the hospital garden, I put my head in my hands and wept.

When my father had failed to emerge from his cottage that morning, the locals had gone in and found him on his bed, stretched out peacefully, as though asleep. They called the ambulance, but it was already too late. The doctor had him sent straight to the morgue. Everyone was devastated. They all agreed what a good man he was. They had been a little wary of him when he first moved to the village, but soon enough they'd come to see him as one of their own. As the villagers sang my father's praises, I sat there cursing myself. What would it have cost me to give him a little more of my time, a little more attention? Yes, perhaps he had shut himself off in some ways, but it wasn't as though I, for my part, had made the slightest effort to get to know him, either.

Once they could see that I had started to regain my composure, the villagers asked me where he was to be buried. I was taken aback by the question, and it must have shown on my face. I'd never thought about it. Or, rather, it had never even occurred to me that my father might die one day. Worse still, my father had rarely crossed my mind over the past few months. After a moment's hesitation, I answered, "I'm sure he'd have had no objection to being buried here. But if it's all right with you, I'd like to have him buried in Isparta, next to my mother." They all agreed it was the right thing to do. We discussed the funeral, and after arranging to set off early the next morning, everyone headed home. Only Selim *Amca* remained. "Come on, you two, you'll be my guests tonight," he said firmly.

"That's very kind of you," said Fırat, "but we wouldn't

want to put you out. We'll stay at a hotel. Besides, we have to get going early in the morning."

"I'll have none of it," Selim *Amca* insisted. "It would be my pleasure. Though if you'd prefer, your father's house is empty, you could always stay there."

We liked the sound of this better. "Of course," I said, "that makes perfect sense." Fırat nodded in agreement.

When we turned on the light in my father's cottage, we could see the entire space from where we stood; it consisted of nothing but a small hallway at the front and a bedroom in the back, a tiny kitchen, and a bathroom. The first thing we noticed was a wooden desk in front of the window in the hallway, with a lamp and a wooden chair. The cottage had little other furniture to speak of: a wooden bench similar to those in the garden, and a coffee table, along with an old kilim on the floor. On the desk stood a stack of notebooks, the kind we used in elementary school, and some pencils. While Fırat went to look around the bedroom and bathroom, I picked up a notebook from the top of the pile and quickly flipped through it. Every page was covered with my father's handwriting. There were eleven notebooks in total, each filled with his penciled scrawling. My father was either trying to improve his handwriting or . . . or what?

I scooped up the pile of notebooks and sat down on the bench. I took the first one from my lap and opened it to the first page. I was dumbfounded. It took me a few moments to pull my wits together and call out to Fırat, who came and sat down next to me. I handed him the notebook.

"Read this," I said to him, still in shock.

Fırat read the title and the first few sentences out loud.

" 'As Lonely as History. There are times when, even in the busiest of crowds, you feel completely alone, as though you are the only person in this entire universe aware of your own existence. If this means that every stone on the path to loneliness has been laid by nobody else but you, then . . . ' " Fırat continued reading silently for a while. After flipping through the rest of the pages, reading the occasional paragraph here and there, we realized that Hasan Vefa Karadağlı's novel had been carefully transcribed, word for word, into this notebook. It continued in the other notebooks, too. And it wasn't just this novel; we soon saw that his next, *It's Love That Stays with You,* had also been copied down word for word. We couldn't believe it, what a strange coincidence. It seemed that over these last years, my father had been reading the same books we had. And clearly the books must have had the same impact on him as they had on us; so much so, in fact, that he had decided to copy them down into these notebooks in order to truly absorb them. The truth was, I never would have believed my father capable of reading such books. Once again, I felt a stab of regret as I thought of how little I had known him. Fırat

scoured the entire house, searching through the books
in the bedroom, but couldn't find a copy of the novels
anywhere. To think that my father had spent the last five
years of his life here, but it was only now, after his death,
that I was finally setting foot in the place myself. Yet no
matter how great my remorse, there was nothing I could
do to make up for it now.

Several of the villagers accompanied us as we set
off early the next morning to take my father's body
to Isparta. It was midday by the time we reached the
graveyard. After the noontime prayers, they performed
the burial rites. More people had come than I expected.
All of my parents' relatives, near and distant, were there,
and their friends, too. Many of them I didn't recognize,
it had been so long since I'd last seen them. But they
all came up to offer their condolences. Faced with their
genuine sorrow, I couldn't help but feel ashamed.

Once the funeral was over, the mourners began to
make their way out of the cemetery. I told Fırat that I
wanted to stay a little longer. Linking his arm in mine, he
stood with me before my parents' graves. The cemetery
was deserted except for one old man who stood quietly
beside us. I turned and looked at him, studying his face.
He seemed familiar, but I couldn't quite place him. He
solemnly approached us and offered his condolences.
I thanked him. I was certain I recognized him from
somewhere, but under the circumstances it seemed

rude to ask him who he was. Sensing the reason for my hesitation, he explained.

"You wouldn't know me, but your father and I were childhood friends. We went to school together. He dropped out after middle school, but I kept studying and went on to university in Izmir. I had to move around a lot because of my job, but your father and I never lost touch. A few years ago I retired and moved back to Isparta. I'd go down to Finike to see your father every now and then, and stay with him for a few days. We'd go fishing together and spend all night talking. We were very close, you see." He sighed.

"It's so good to meet one of my father's friends," I said warmly. "I only wish we'd met earlier."

He handed me a business card. "We run a foundation in Istanbul. Come by sometime if you can and I'll tell you a thing or two about your father." He smiled.

When we read the name on the business card, Fırat and I cried out almost in unison: "My God, I can't believe it!"

The old man standing before us was none other than Hasan Vefa Karadağlı, our beloved author.

"Of course, that's how we recognize you," said Fırat. "From the photo on your books."

"It's truly an honor to meet you," I gushed. "Honestly, though, it's hard to believe that you and my father were childhood friends. We're huge fans of your work. I have to say, your novels have touched our lives. Now I understand why my father copied them into those notebooks."

The man was older than he appeared in his author photo; they must have used an earlier picture of him for the book jacket. Looking at his face, I could tell how deeply my father's death had upset him.

"You're wrong about that, dear," Hasan Vefa said, drawing closer to me and looking me straight in the eyes. He took a deep breath before he continued. "Your father didn't copy my books into his notebooks. On the contrary, it's his words that fill those novels."

At first we thought he was joking, but his demeanor suggested otherwise. "These last few years, your father poured his heart out into those notebooks there in that house in Finike. Whenever I stopped by, he'd read me what he'd written, and I found his words to be so touching, so true. I kept trying to get him to publish them until eventually he agreed. But on one condition. 'I don't want anything published under my name,' he told me. 'The last thing I want to do is ruin the peaceful life I've made for myself here. So if you really want to publish them, do it under your own name and then you can deal with all the hassle that comes with it.' 'That's fine,' I told him, 'but I have one condition, too: If they sell, all the money will go toward helping young writers, we won't touch a single *kuruş*.' We agreed, and in just two years, we had both novels published. Just as I had expected, they became bestsellers, and as promised, we used the money to set up a foundation in Istanbul. It's already done so much to help young writers," he said, beaming.

Fırat and I listened, our mouths agape.

"Don't forget to stop by the foundation," he said as he shook our hands and bade us farewell. "And by the way, your father left those notebooks to you. He didn't want me to tell you any of this while he was still alive, and he made me swear not to tell anyone but you. Those notebooks are precious. They're much more than just words, they're his final testament to you, and to people everywhere." And with that, he turned around and walked away.

I looked over at my father's grave and then at Fırat. Kneeling down, I scooped up a handful of earth, and as I ran it through my fingers, I made this promise: I would leave shame behind, and regret. From here on in, I would live my life differently.

A MAGNIFICENT ENDING

I t had been a long city council meeting, but as he made his way home, he could barely contain his excitement. He stepped through the open gate to find his mother in her usual spot in the garden, tending to her vegetables. He threw his arms around her and planted a kiss on her cheek. She was so startled that she would have fallen to the ground had her son not been holding up her weary body.

"What's gotten into you?" she asked. "You almost scared me to death. You certainly are in good spirits today!"

"I've got news for you," he replied. "I'm going to America for a conference. The council chose *me*."

Her eyes misted over with pride—the same pride she had felt when he had left for medical school and then again when he came back to work as a doctor. She had been pregnant with him when they killed her husband. It was only after years of hardship and persecution that things finally took a turn for the better. By the time her son was old enough for school, the city council and the neighborhood assemblies had established new schools that taught in Kurdish, their mother tongue. And it was in one such school that she herself had finally learned to read and write. Meanwhile, here on the banks of the Tigris, where ancient civilizations once flourished, residents had been encouraged to take up farming, with parcels of land allocated to any and all who wished to till the soil. New irrigation canals brought the waters of the Tigris directly to their fields and gardens. Each of the neighborhood assemblies had established its own cooperative, and through these producers began to sell their goods directly to one another and throughout the region as well. These same cooperatives had helped to revive animal farming and traditional crafts while also bringing more and more tourists to the area. As each of the towns in the district grew self-sufficient, residents began to hold their heads high, and rightly so. The whole community had been mobilized in the effort to end the legacy of corruption, bribery, theft, drugs, and prostitution that had cast such a dark shadow over their past. Great progress had been made. Determined that the younger generation should be raised with strong moral and political values, everyone had come together, introducing new measures for the greater good in the neighborhood assemblies. Knowing how hard it would be to rid themselves of their old habits, they cultivated patience, building their new lives one brick at a time. They were now on the verge of making unemployment and poverty a thing of the past. Their goal was to create a model of social economy that was fully democratic. They had already overcome a number of obstacles and, in this first half of our century, established a system that set an example for the rest of the world. Through an initiative that harnessed solar and wind power, they supplied the city with green energy and introduced urban development policies that respected both nature and history. Health services were free of charge and accessible to all, and the judicial system was fair and unbiased. People's assemblies worked on the principle of direct democracy, adopting an open-minded approach to issues such as gender, faith, and lifestyle. All this had attracted international attention and brought in accolades from far and wide. These achievements had paved the way for social peace not only in their region but also throughout the land; and now, despite its painful history, the country had become a model for peaceful coexistence, earning it the admiration of the entire world.

After graduating from medical school, her son returned to his hometown, where he was appointed by the council to work at the public health center. Already a familiar face beloved by all, he soon proved an excellent doctor and gained a reputation for being helpful and hardworking as well as modest.

At the annual council elections, he was chosen first as a councillor and then as the council's cospokesperson. Though he devoted himself to his civic duties, his enthusiasm for his work as a doctor was undiminished. All his life, he had strived to live up to the example set by the father and uncle he had never met, and now, by serving his community, he was delighted to finally have the chance to do so.

Harvard University had invited the city council to send a delegate to Cambridge to give a talk about its successful model of local governance. And now, at today's meeting, the council had decided that he should be the one to go.

Though the conference was not for another month, his excitement was palpable. For the first time in his twenty-eight years, he would be going to America. Other than a short stay in London to attend a language course, he had never been abroad. The idea of representing his people at such a prestigious university, to talk about all they had achieved, only made the prospect that much more thrilling. And since being chosen, he'd been crafting the perfect speech, one that was thorough yet concise. Before he left, he gave his talk in front of the city council and it was met with great applause.

From the local airport, just outside of town, he would fly to Istanbul, and from there on to America. The morning of his departure, he asked his friend Bawer, who was driving him to the airport, to stop at the cemetery on the way. He had gathered some wildflowers from the garden, which he now placed on as many graves as he could. The last of his flowers he laid upon two graves that stood side by side. With a heavy heart and a note of pride in his voice, he murmured, "May you rest in peace." On the headstones were engraved the names of his father, Ahmet Tunç, and his uncle, Mehmet Tunç.

At the airport, Bawer gave the doctor a long hug.

"Have a safe trip, Bêkes," he said. "Take in all the sights you can. You're traveling for all of us, you know."

Bêkes had never been short of people who cared for him. He had grown up as a child of the people and had always been surrounded by so much love that it drew a striking contrast with his name—Bêkes, "the orphan." As Bêkes the doctor waved goodbye to his friend, the scorching Cizre sun reached its peak, marking yet another day of this new life on the banks of the Tigris.

NOTES

The Turkish language is peppered with various forms of address, for which direct equivalents rarely exist in English: *Bacı,* meaning "sister," is often used by men in left-wing groups to address their female comrades. *Abi,* meaning "older brother," and *abla,* meaning "older sister," are also frequently used to address a man or a woman more senior in age, indicating both respect and familiarity. *Amca,* meaning "maternal uncle," is also a familiar form of address for an older man, while *teyze,* meaning "maternal aunt," is the equivalent for a woman. *Ana,* meaning "mother," can be used together with the proper name as a form of address, indicating both respect and familiarity. *Baba* means "father." *Bey/Hanım* are the equivalents of *Mr./Mrs.* and are used with the person's first name; their usage denotes a more formal relationship. *Usta,* "master," is a form of address used for craftsmen or people who are skilled at their trade.

Seher

Seher: The name *Seher* means "dawn." When asked by the *Cumhuriyet* newspaper, in an interview conducted from prison, why he had chosen "Seher" as the name for the main character in the title story of the book, Selahattin Demirtaş said, "Dawn marks the first moments when light emerges from darkness. Dawn represents hope, revives itself anew each day. Darkness thinks itself eternal, and just as it believes it has defeated the light, dawn deals the first blow. This is the moment that brings an end to darkness and marks the beginning of light."

bayram: This refers to either of the two main Muslim festivals—*Eid al-Fitr* (in Turkish *Şeker Bayramı,* or *Ramazan Bayramı,* the Festival of Sweets or Ramadan Festival), a three-day festival to mark the end of the month of Ramadan, or *Eid al-Adha* (in Turkish *Kurban*

Bayramı, Sacrifice Festival), a four-day festival in honor of
Ibrahim's willingness to sacrifice his son to Allah. As well
as being important religious festivals, these *bayrams* are
major public holidays in Turkey.

Adana/Çukurova: A major city in south-central
Anatolia, Adana is the largest city in the Çukurova
region, the fertile agricultural heartland of Turkey and
an area closely associated with the works of Nobel-
nominated author and human rights activist Yaşar Kemal
(1923–2015).

Nazan the Cleaning Lady

Ankara/Mamak: Ankara is the capital city of Turkey,
located in the region of central Anatolia. Mamak is a
metropolitan district of the capital and home to the
infamous Mamak Military Prison.

gecekondu: Literally meaning "put up at night," a *gecekondu*
is a dwelling erected illegally overnight on empty land on
the outskirts of cities.

Madımak: Also known as the Sivas Massacre, this refers
to the murder of thirty-five artists and intellectuals,

mostly Alevis, a religious minority, who burned to death when right-wing nationalists set fire to the Madımak Hotel where they were staying while in Sivas for a festival in 1993.

Kızılay Square: The main public square in Ankara. The name Kızılay (Red Crescent) was given to the square when the headquarters of the Turkish Red Crescent was built there. The square has since been renamed twice, first to *Hürriyet Meydanı* (Liberty Square), after the military coup of 1960, and later to *15 Temmuz Kızılay Milli İrade Meydanı* (July 15 Kızılay National Will Square), after the attempted coup that took place on July 15, 2016. Despite these name changes, the public continues to refer to it as simply Kızılay. Located in the center of Ankara, it is the main gathering point for protests in the city.

It's Not What You Think

Karlıova: A district in the Bingöl province in eastern Anatolia.

Alaçatı: A traditional town on the Aegean coast, Alaçatı has in recent years developed into a popular and upmarket tourist destination.

lahmacun: Sometimes referred to as "Turkish pizza," this is a food made of thin dough topped with spicy ground meat and served with parsley and lemon.

Olympos: An ancient Lycian city on the Mediterranean coast of southwest Turkey, Olympos is now a popular tourist destination and known as a bohemian hangout.

Greetings to Those Dark Eyes

Muş: A province in the majority-Kurdish region of eastern Anatolia.

"My darling girl, don't let anyone harm you, not even a single eyelash. Be strong,": In July 2015, Çilem Doğan was arrested for killing her husband, who had been trying to force her into prostitution. In response to the letters of solidarity she received while in prison, Doğan wrote: "May not a single of your eyelashes fall to the ground," a line that became a mantra for the feminist movement in Turkey.

Edirne F-Type High-Security Prison: The prison in which the author, Selahattin Demirtaş, was interned at the time of writing this book. The decision to incarcerate him in a prison approximately 1,700 kilometers (1,056 miles) from his home in Diyarbakır has been criticized as a deliberate form of additional punishment for both Demirtaş and his family.

A Letter to the Prison Letter-Reading Committee

İlhami Algör: Born in 1955 in Suriçi, Istanbul, Algör is the author of several novellas in Turkish, as well as a nonfiction book about the 1938 massacre of the local population of Dersim, a city in eastern Turkey from which his family hails. His work features the recurrent question "What is the point/issue?"—a purposefully vague and philosophical question that usually goes unanswered, representing the ever-changing, elusive nature of "the point/issue" at hand.

Arif Sağ: Born in 1945 in Aşkale, Erzurum, Sağ is an Alevi singer and a *bağlama* (a traditional string instrument) virtuoso. He also served as a member of parliament for the Social Democratic Populist Party from 1987 to 1991. He survived the 1993 Sivas Massacre (see "Madımak" in "Nazan the Cleaning Lady").

Diyarbakır: One of the largest cities in the majority-Kurdish region of southeastern Anatolia, Diyarbakır is the author's hometown.

"the co-leadership system didn't yet exist back then, of course": The Peoples' Democratic Party, to which the author belongs, follows a dual-leadership system, with all positions of leadership filled by two people: one male, one female.

Kebab Halabi

Kebab Halabi: Halabi, taken from the Arabic, denotes an origin from Aleppo (*Halab*) in Syria. *Kebab Halabi* is the name of a dish—a lamb kebab served with tomato sauce and Aleppo pepper. The original Turkish title of this story ("*Halep Ezmesi*," translating literally as "Aleppo Puree") does not appear to be an actual dish but instead lends itself to interpretation.

Hatay: Also known as Antakya (ancient Antioch), Hatay is a historically multicultural city located in the Mediterranean region, close to the Turkish-Syrian border.

künefe: A baked dessert made of layers of shredded wheat soaked in syrup and filled with a soft, unsalted cheese.

As Lonely as History

The book titles mentioned in this story are lines taken from the poetry of Murathan Mungan, a prominent contemporary poet, author, and playwright. An outspoken advocate for human rights, Mungan was born in Istanbul; his family hails from Mardin in southeastern Turkey.

Isparta: A province in southwestern Turkey, approximately 150 kilometers (93 miles) north of Antalya, famous for its rose cultivation.

Finike: A district in the Antalya Province, located on the Mediterranean coast in southern Turkey.

Beyoğlu: A district on the European side of Istanbul, Beyoğlu is a popular area for shopping and nightlife.

Fikirtepe: The neighborhood of Fikirtepe, which is located in the district of Kadıköy on the Asian side of Istanbul, has been a particularly controversial urban renewal site in recent years. Urban renewal in Istanbul began after the Marmara earthquake of 1999, presumably to ensure that all buildings are earthquake-proof. However, the process has been criticized because it effectively displaces local residents while filling the pockets of contractors and construction companies.

A Magnificent Ending

The sociopolitical developments in this story, set in the near future, are a reflection of the political goals of the Peoples' Democratic Party, to which the author belongs.

The main character in this story, Bêkes, is based on a real person of the same name. During the military curfew on the city of Cizre (a majority-Kurdish town and district in southeastern Anatolia, on the Turkish border with Syria) in 2015–16, Bêkes's father and uncle were among the many killed when security forces stormed the basements in which hundreds were sheltering from the fighting. The name literally means "he who has no one"—an orphan—and was given to him by his father before he died.

Bêkes's father, Orhan Tunç, and uncle, Mehmet Tunç (co-chair of the Cizre People's Assembly), were buried in the Nalaro Cemetery in the district of Şırnak, rather than in their hometown of Cizre, due to the ongoing blockade there. They were interred in a mass burial along with twenty-eight others who were killed during the blockade. A few months after the burial, there were reports that the area around the cemetery had come under attack by state forces and that the cemetery and its environs were damaged by fire. Unlike the Islamic tradition of wrapping the bodies in a shroud for burial, many of the bodies were buried in coffins so that families could later have them exhumed and reinterred in Cizre. From the story we can assume that the cemetery mentioned is in Cizre and that the bodies have therefore been moved.

In 1917 Virginia and Leonard Woolf started The Hogarth Press armed only with a hand-press and a determination to publish the newest, most inspiring writing. They went on to publish some of the twentieth century's most significant writers.

Inspired by their example, Hogarth was relaunched in 2012 as an adventurous fiction imprint with an accent on the pleasures of storytelling and a keen awareness of the world. Our novels are published from London and New York.

In 2015 we celebrated Shakespeare's 400th year with the Hogarth Shakespeare series. Margaret Atwood, Edward St Aubyn, Tracy Chevalier, Gillian Flynn, Howard Jacobson, Jo Nesbo, Anne Tyler and Jeanette Winterson were asked to choose a play and reimagine it for a contemporary readership. The novels have been published in 24 languages around the world.

A Place for Us marked the start of our collaboration with Sarah Jessica Parker. The award-winning actor, producer and honorary chair of the American Library Association's book club was elected in 2009 by the Obama administration to the President's Committee on the Arts and the Humanities. As part of the Hogarth editorial team in New York Ms Parker selects and acquires works of literary fiction that reflect her own taste as a reader. She is directly involved in the editorial and publishing process, with her vision providing the editorial foundation for each publication. *Dawn* is the latest in our collaboration with Ms Parker.